RESCUED

JESSICA GRAYSON

ARIA WINTER

Purple Fall
Publishing

DEDICATION

To my husband: You are not just my husband, you are my best friend and my rock. Thank you for all your love and support. I love you more than words can ever say.

-Jessica Grayson

CHAPTER 1

VIOLET

My pulse pounds in my ears as I race through the forest. The last of the sun's rays filters in through the trees, their red, pine-like needles casting a sinister orange-red glow on the snow-covered landscape around them.

Blood drips down my front onto the snow, staining a path our A'kai masters will undoubtedly follow.

"Hurry, Elain!" I yell over my shoulder.

A piercing scream behind me draws my attention, and I spin to find her lying face down in the snow. She curls onto her side, her expression twisted in agony as she rubs at her ankle.

I rush to her, tugging at her arm to help her stand.

She tries to walk, but stumbles forward. "I can't, Violet. My ankle's twisted."

I pull her arm over my shoulder and hold onto her waist, supporting her weight as I drag her beside me. "Yes, you can. We can do this."

We push through the dense bramble as branches grasp at us like wiry, skeletal hands, tangling in my long brown hair and catching on my clothing.

Tears stream down Elain's face. "I'm just slowing you down."

My heart hammers in my chest, sharp pains stabbing through my sides toward my burning lungs. They can't be far behind us. "Come on, Elain," I grit through my teeth, pulling her along. "We have to keep going."

The sound of rushing water ahead echoes through the forest, sparking hope deep inside me.

Our A'kai masters can't swim.

I learned this when they had us avoid crossing a river a few days ago, arguing that if they fell in, they would drown.

"If we can reach the water, we can lose them. It can't be that much farther. We can make it."

A thunderous roar echoes through the forest as our masters give voice to their rage.

A blast of light catches the corner of my eye a moment before blinding pain rips through my forearm around her shoulder.

Another blast follows quickly behind it, and Elain jerks forward, dropping to the ground in a crumpled heap. The flesh on her back is charred from the blaster hit, matching the skin on my arm.

I grip my blaster, firing two shots randomly into the forest in a pitiful attempt to stave them off.

I fall to my knees beside Elain, turning her onto her back. Her eyelids flutter open and closed as she stares up at me. "You have to leave me," she rasps. "I'm not going to make it."

Tears escape my lashes and stream down my cheeks. "No." My voice quavers. "I can't."

The harsh sound of crunching snow and ice seizes my

attention, and I lift my head to see our A'kai masters racing toward us with inhuman speed.

I fire another two shots, each missing their mark entirely as the A'kai easily dodge them.

I glance down at Elain, her face pale and drawn as she stares up at me. "Go," she urges. "You have to leave me."

A broken sob escapes my lips as I take her hand, dropping my forehead to hers. I brush her long, red hair back from her face, as her warm brown eyes stare up into mine, full of tears. "Please," I beg, my voice shaking. "We have to go, Elain. Please, get up."

"I can't, Violet," she barely manages. She palms the blaster in her hand and fixes me with a firm look. "Go. I'll hold them off."

I hesitate, but she pushes at me. "Now, Violet!"

Another blast of light rushes toward me, and I twist to the side, barely avoiding the hit as I race through the forest.

Glancing over my shoulder, I watch as Elain hits one of the A'kai, and he drops like a stone to the forest floor.

I break out from beneath the tree canopy, the sun's golden rays momentarily blinding, and stop short at the edge of a cliff wall. My eyes widen as I peer over the side at the terrifying drop to the raging river below.

Several more shots ring out. Elain releases a pain filled cry, then falls silent.

Without warning, one of the A'kai crashes through the trees into the clear space between me and the forest. He stops short, his lips pulled back in a feral snarl, and bares his fangs. His nails extend into sharp claws. His glowing, green eyes turn raven-black.

A trail of black blood drips down from his snow-white hairline. His normally pale-green skin is flushed dark in anger. He is like a Vampire of Terran myth as he stalks closer —a predator closing in on its prey.

With each step he takes, I back away, closer to the edge, holding my injured arm to my chest. "There is nowhere to run," he says darkly.

My heart threatens to leap from the cage of my chest as I dart a glance over my shoulder to the water rushing below, weighing the decision to jump or surrender.

"Your species is weak, Terran," Leron sneers. "You will not survive that fall."

His gaze flicks to the two puncture wounds on my neck, and the bright-red drops of blood falling in the snow by my feet. His nostrils flare and he licks his lips. "Step away from that ledge. It would be such a waste of a delicious meal if you were to fall to your death."

He moves closer and I step back, only a hair's breadth from the edge of the cliff. His people are touch telepaths. Able to enter and manipulate someone's mind through the simple act of touch. I know that if I allow him to place his hand on me, I'll be lost.

He'll enslave my mind to his, forcing me to surrender to him. Dark memories of all the times he invaded my consciousness in the *R'ugol*—the forced mind link—surface, and fear ripples down my spine.

I lift my face toward the blue sky above. The sun's golden rays filter in through thick, gray clouds, illuminating a circle of light all around me. Closing my eyes, I bask in the radiance of its warmth, steeling myself for the choice I must make.

I cannot go back; I refuse to surrender.

"Come here," Leron snaps, drawing my attention back to him, as he slowly advances.

My eyes lock onto his, their obsidian depths burning with rage as an evil snarl curls his lips, revealing his sharpened canines.

I won't be taken again. I choose death.

My pulse pounds in my ears, drowning out all other noise as the space between each heartbeat spreads out like an eternity. Spreading my arms wide, I close my eyes, and allow myself to fall back.

"No!" A deafening roar splits the air.

My eyes snap open, and the world shifts into slow motion as a man with violet skin, short, dark hair, and dragonfly wings dives toward me from above with his arms outstretched, trying to save me.

He's Aerilon, I realize. I've seen his kind before.

His golden eyes are wide with panic as I reach for him. Our fingers brush and warmth spreads across my skin and over my palm from the light contact a moment before he grasps my hand firmly, and pulls me into his arms.

He twists beneath me, and his back slams into the water, taking the brunt of the impact as we plunge into the icy river. The current is brutal and unforgiving, ripping me from my savior's iron embrace, threatening to swallow me whole as it drags me downstream.

Kicking my legs, I swim to the surface, breaking through and gasping for air as the violent torrent threatens to pull me under again.

The Aerilon surfaces, and reaches for me again. "Take my hand!"

I extend my arm, but only the tips of our fingers brush. "You're too far away! I—"

My words cut off as the current drags me under and my head hits a rock. Darkness creeps in around the edges of my vision and I blink several times, struggling to swim back up. My heart hammers as my lungs burn from lack of oxygen, desperate for air.

A hand grips my forearm and pulls me up from the depths.

Coughing and sputtering, I draw in great gulping breaths

as I break through the surface. The Aerilon gathers me in his arms as the current dips and swirls around several large boulders, spinning us wildly.

The turbulent water pulls us to another and he twists, trying to avoid it, only to be caught by another torrent and slammed against the boulder. A pained cry rips from his throat as his back hits the rock with a sickening crunch.

Black liquid blooms in the water around us, and I realize it's his blood.

Despite his obvious pain, he holds tightly to me and swims us to the shore. He pulls me to his chest, carrying me up onto the riverbank. Gently, he sets me down against a large tree trunk as I shiver uncontrollably.

Quickly, he removes the cloak from around his shoulders and hands it to me. He releases a strange string of syllables with a soft trilling sound at the end.

I blink several times in confusion. "What did you say?"

He repeats the words and the odd sounds, but none of it makes sense. "I can't understand you."

He frowns and walks toward me. Instinctively, I throw my arms up as if to shield myself, my body conditioned to expect a beating from my masters. The movement makes sharp pain shoot through my arm from my injury.

Instantly, he stills. He raises both hands out before him in a placating gesture and points to my left ear—the side of my head that hit the rock underwater.

I reach behind my ear and feel for the translator the slavers injected just under the skin, but I feel nothing. When I pull my hand away, I notice a small amount of blood on my first two fingers.

My rescuer's golden eyes widen in concern as we stare at each other helplessly.

Without a translator, I have no hope of understanding him.

He holds the cloak out to me again and I take it, surprised that it's completely dry despite the fact that we just came out of the water.

I'm so miserable, I start to pull off my wet clothing when I realize he's staring at me, his mouth gaping open. "Could you please turn around?" I murmur through chattering teeth.

When he doesn't respond right away, I make a circular motion with my finger, gesturing for him to turn around.

He blinks several times before understanding dawns across his features, and he turns his back to me.

I sigh heavily. It seems the translator must work both ways. It helped me understand him and him understand me. Now that it's gone, neither of us can understand each other. I hope he can fix this somehow because it will be awful to spend the rest of my life lost in space, not being able to talk to anyone.

A cold wind whips around my form, pulling me back from my despairing thoughts. A small hiss of pain escapes me when I move my arm to change into the cloak. The material isn't exactly warm, but at least it's dry.

He turns and kneels before me, his attention locked on the arm I cradle to my chest. He releases another odd series of words and trills, but it's easy to read the concern on his face as he gestures to my injury.

In the icy water, I'd managed to push the pain to the back of my mind, but now the burning sensation is almost unbearable.

Shakily, I extend my arm to him.

His larger hands trace over my injured forearm, taking great care to be gentle as he assesses my wound.

I allow my eyes to wander over his pale-violet skin, elvish ears, and short, black hair. He's dressed in some sort of dark, form-fitting uniform that only accentuates his broad shoulders and does little to hide the bulging muscles of his body beneath.

He's gorgeous. With his dragonfly appearing wings he looks like a Fae Prince. The aristocratic features of his cheekbones, brow, and nose, lend him a regal appearance, but it's his golden eyes which captivate me most as he stares down at me in concern.

One of my close friends was a doctor. I've seen that look before. It's bad. It must be, judging by his expression. Worry tightens my chest, but I force myself to push it back down.

This guy saved me, but the A'kai are still out here somewhere. We need to hide or at least find some sort of shelter before nightfall. I'm not sure how to communicate this to him, but I have to try.

I place a hand over my chest and meet his golden eyes evenly. "I'm Violet." I reach across and rest my palm on his chest. "What is your name?"

"Al'iro," he replies.

"Ah-leer-roh," I sound it out slowly, making sure I've said it right.

He nods and then sounds out my name in return. "Vy-oh-let."

I smile brightly at him. "That's perfect."

He returns my smile with a devastatingly handsome one of his own. My heart stops, however, when I notice the two rows of sharp fangs that line his mouth.

His expression quickly falls into one of concern, and I note the kindness behind his eyes as he studies me. It gives me pause. My gaze darts to his wings, remembering how he injured them while shielding me from harm.

Perhaps, it's because of this that my first instinct isn't to flinch when he tenderly tucks a stray tendril of hair behind my ear. Despite his sharp teeth and black claws, I don't feel as if he would hurt me.

His gaze holds mine intently and a hot flush creeps up my neck to my face and cheeks. He reaches out to touch my face, studying me in concern.

"It's called 'blushing,' " I tell him, even though he can't understand me. "I don't normally blush around men, but you're really handsome... the most gorgeous man I've ever seen, to be honest. Not to mention the whole knight-in-shining armor thing you have going on."

He blinks several times and then tips his head to the side to regard me.

I swallow thickly. "Sorry. I just... have a tendency to ramble when I'm nervous, you know. Not that you're scary or anything. It's just the opposite, in fact, but I—"

I stop abruptly as his head snaps toward the woods. I still as he scans the forest as if searching for something.

Memories of Elain surface in my mind, and I swallow against the sudden lump in my throat as I force myself to push down my sadness. I can't let my emotions distract me. Not now. I have to focus on staying alive.

Standing at alert, Al'iro's golden eyes stare into the forest, a dark expression on his face. Cautiously, I move up behind him and touch his arm, drawing his attention to me. "Do you think we're being followed? Do you see anyone else out there?"

A menacing growl echoes through the woods, and he goes completely still. His nostrils flare as he tips up his chin, scenting the air. He says something else I can't possibly hope to understand, but when his gaze flashes to mine, I know it must be serious.

He gathers me to his chest. He flexes his wings but hisses in pain, quickly lowering them again. Worried eyes meet my own, and I realize his wings are so badly injured, he can't fly.

Another growl sounds nearby, and I reach for my blaster, only to find it gone. Gritting my teeth, I curse under my breath in frustration. I probably lost it in the river.

Al'iro spins toward the noise, pulling me behind him as if to shield me. A low growl rumbles deep in his chest. His black claws extend into sharp talons as he stares into the dark woods, baring his fangs.

I'd probably think he was terrifying if I didn't realize that he's trying to protect me. I'm really glad he's on my side right now. I can use all the help I can get. My gaze travels over his injured wings, black blood dried and crusted across one of the tendons. He saved me when it would have been easier to let me get hurt instead. I trust that he's not going to harm me.

A flash of movement in the forest catches my attention. Ice cold fear floods my veins as a heavily muscled man with golden skin, slightly pointed ears, and glowing, yellow eyes steps out of the woods. He levels a dark glare at Al'iro as he speaks in a series of guttural growls. His nostrils flare as he scents the wind and leans to one side, trying to peer past Al'iro to me.

Al'iro moves quickly to block his view, releasing a low growl of warning.

The man's lips pull back in an answering snarl, revealing sharp fangs.

He stills, and whips his head to one side. Al'iro does this as well. Their eyes are transfixed on something deep in the forest that I cannot see.

The man speaks in his strange, harsh language again, but this time his tone sounds even angrier than before.

Lightning fast, he changes before my eyes. His entire form shifting into a brown wolf, but several times larger than any I've ever seen on Terra. I draw in a shaking breath as I stare at a monster straight out of a nightmare.

"Oh my god, it's a werewolf," I murmur to myself. Slowly, I reach out and grasp Al'iro's forearm, tugging him back toward me as I address the wolf. "Please, don't eat us. I promise you, we'd taste terrible."

CHAPTER 2

AL'IRO

Dakor's jaw drops as he stares at her incredulously. "I'm not going to *eat* you. I am here to *save* you." He turns to me, his lips twisted in a feral snarl. "Give the female to me."

Fierce protectiveness floods my system. I will die before I let him touch her. A low growl rises in my throat. "No."

He stalks closer in challenge. "Give her to me. Our pack will keep her safe from the A'kai."

"Why should I trust you won't hurt her?"

He narrows his eyes. "Do you truly believe me or my kind would ever harm a female? They are life givers—favored of the Moon Goddess. They are to be cherished and protected."

He tells me these things as if they were common knowledge, but I have never heard this about his people. I have only had dealings with his pack a handful of times before now, and none of them pleasant exchanges. They are savage and aggressive; preferring to roam and hunt the land in their four-legged beast forms.

They hate the V'loryn and by extension, us as well. They have a tentative truce with the Mosaurans, but that does not include our people.

My nostrils flare as the acrid scent of her fear fills the air. Fierce protectiveness fills me as I glare at Dakor, second in command of his pack. "Go cherish and protect someone else. You are scaring her. Leave now, before I end you."

Indignation burns in his glowing yellow eyes. "How do I know it is not *you* that she fears? After all, you and your kind have allied yourself with the V'loryns."

"What quarrel do you have with them?"

"Everyone knows they are as dangerous as the A'kai," he grinds out. "They hide their savagery behind stoic masks, but deep down they are the same and you know it, Al'iro."

"You are wrong. The V'loryns are nothing like the A'kai."

He lowers his head, staring at me through dark brows. "My people have long memories. We have not forgotten that the V'loryn Empire decimated our world when we refused to submit to their rule."

"That was over two thousand cycles ago," I counter. "They are different now."

Dakor tips up his chin. "So you claim."

Violet tugs on my arm, trying to pull me back to her as she speaks under her breath. "Look, I know you're really big and strong, but I think we need to run, Al'iro."

Despite our situation, I cannot help but puff my chest out with pride.

She continues. "This guy is really big and really scary, and I'm not sure you can take him in a fight."

My chest quickly deflates at her words, my pride now wounded beyond saving. *Does she think I am not strong enough to protect her?*

Amusement dances behind Dakor's eyes as his lips curl up in a smirk. "You see? Even *she* believes you are too weak to keep her safe. She obviously recognizes which of us is the superior male."

A growl rises in my throat at his taunting words, but I stop as she quickly steps around me, moving to my side.

She takes my hand, squeezing it gently. She lifts her eyes to mine. "I know you can't understand my words, but you're going to have to trust me."

I blink several times. *Why does she think I cannot understand her?*

Her gaze sweeps to the Lycaon and she lowers her voice. "I watched a nature documentary once about wolves. I think they said you need to stare them down; don't break eye contact so you can establish dominance... or something to that effect."

Despite the strong smell of her fear, she forces herself to stand before Dakor, staring at him, unblinking.

This female is brave.

He tilts his head and narrows his eyes, studying her with a look somewhere between confusion and disbelief.

Her small brow furrowing deeply. "Or... maybe that was some other animal. I don't remember now. Why didn't I pay closer attention to that stupid nature show?"

Dakor takes a step closer. "What is wrong with you, female? Did you not hear everything I just said? I am trying to save you from this Aerilon scum that would deliver you straight into the hands of the V'loryns."

"Oh, god," she says, gripping my hand with a strength I did not realize her people possessed. "I think I've just made it even worse. He looks *really* mad now. Maybe if we stop staring at him, he'll lose interest and go away."

He frowns and his gaze slides to mine. "Please tell me she simply does not have a translator, and not that her mind has been broken."

I blink several times, surprised by his statement. Perhaps he really does mean her no harm. "She lost her translator in the river." I dart a glance at my wrist and curse under my breath. I must have lost my wrist communicator to the icy water as well.

His ears flick back toward the woods, and he jerks his head in that direction, growling low. "There are three more A'kai nearby. Fly her away from here. Quickly."

Instinctively, I try to spread my wings. Sharp pain tears across my back along the tendons, and I grit my teeth against the pain. "My wings are damaged. I cannot fly."

"Then, you'll have to run. My pack and I will buy you time." His lips pull back in a feral snarl, revealing two rows of sharp fangs, his eyes fixed on something deep in the forest I cannot see. "If you harm her, I will end you," he threatens.

My brow furrows as his gaze meets mine. He truly does want to keep her safe. "We share the same goal," I tell him. "I want only to protect her."

He dips his chin in a firm nod. "Go. Now. While you can." He turns his gaze back out to the woods as he lowers his head, baring his fangs in a defensive stance. "They are coming."

Without warning, an A'kai bursts out of the forest.

Dakor jumps into his path, and they clash in a vicious mesh of fangs and claws.

Three more Lycaons join the fight, rending flesh from bone as they tear into the A'kai.

Movement in the corner of my eye captures my attention just as another one charges toward us in attack.

I gather Violet tight to my chest and break into a run. My pulse pounds in my ears as I race through the forest. I have to lose him. And fast. My people normally fly; we do not run. I cannot maintain this speed for very long.

Violet looks over my shoulder and gasps.

I glance back and notice two A'kai chasing after us.

The snow is soft, like shifting sand beneath my feet, making it difficult to keep ahead of them. The sounds of their pursuit grow louder. I don't have to look behind me to know they are close.

My muscles burn with exertion as we break through the forest and into a clearing. Up ahead, I see a ledge, with a great valley spread out below it.

I look to either side, but there is no way to go but straight toward it.

Violet tenses in my arms as I race toward the edge of the cliff. "What are you doing?" she cries out, her fear scent so strong it is nearly overwhelming as she clings to me with terror in her eyes.

Without breaking speed, I tighten my hold on her as I race to the edge and leap off the side.

A terrified scream rips from her throat as we plummet toward the forest below.

Blinding pain sears across every nerve ending along my back as I snap my wings open, halting our descent. It takes every bit of my strength to keep them extended as we glide out over the valley beneath us.

I catch a current, struggling to keep us upright. I cannot flap my wings. The agony is too great. Gritting my teeth, I force myself to focus through the intense pain that threatens to render me unconscious.

The A'kai roar behind us in anger; the sound echoing across the valley.

A sea of snow-capped trees spreads out below us, thick and impenetrable. I cannot land here without risking hurting both of us.

With great effort, I dip my left wing, making a slow arc toward a clearing in the far distance. "Hold tight," I grind out. "This will be a rough landing."

As if she somehow knows what I'm saying, she wraps her arms tighter around my neck.

I drift down low over the woods until we reach the clear expanse of ice and snow. My wings shake with effort as I try to control our descent. The ground races beneath us a moment before I touch down.

My boots slide on the ice, and I stumble forward, twisting onto my back at the last second before we slam to the ground, shielding Violet from the force of the impact. I release an agonized roar as pain explodes across my back and wings.

Violet quickly moves off me as I lie in the snow, panting heavily as every nerve ending along my back and wings burns as if on fire. I fix my gaze on the blue sky overhead, willing the pain to calm.

She drops to her knees and cups my cheek, turning my face to hers. "Oh, god, are you all right?"

"I'll live," I rasp.

She blinks down at me. "I hope that means 'yes.' "

I nod, and she gasps. "You can understand me?"

I nod again.

"And that other guy… that wolf… he understood me?"

I give her another affirmatory nod and she narrows her eyes. "Well, thanks a lot for letting me know." She sighs. "Here I was rambling on about establishing dominance and stuff… giving away our plan, and you just let me keep talking."

As she continues, I stare at her, transfixed. Even angry… she is the most beautiful female I have ever seen.

She sighs. "But I guess I can't really stay mad at you now, can I? Not after you injured your beautiful wings to save me."

A smile curves my mouth at her compliment of my wings, glad that she finds them beautiful despite their current state. An Aerilon male's wings are important in attracting a female.

18

A pink flush blooms across her cheeks and the bridge of her nose. I remember her telling me the first time this happened that it was a 'blush,' because she finds me attractive.

My smile widens and the color across her face goes from pink to red.

Violet is the most stunning female I have ever beheld. Her brown hair falls around her shoulders in long, silken waves. Her eyes are a vivid, striking shade somewhere between golden-brown and green, depending upon the light as it hits them.

Her face is heart-shaped, and I notice a light dusting of tiny, pigmented spots across the bridge of her nose and cheeks. I have never seen these before, but then again, I have only seen four other Terrans besides her.

She is a lovely and delicate creature. Despite my pain, I am completely enthralled. I thought only Aerilon females possessed such charming features, but it seems I was wrong.

She averts her gaze as if embarrassed. "Um... do you think you can stand?"

I nod. Drawing in a deep and steeling breath, I force myself to sit up, gritting my teeth in agony as I do. Because I've been lying on the ice, the pain is not as intense as it originally was, but it is still there.

I'm careful as I stand, trying to keep my wings as still as possible, hoping to avoid another flare of pain. The dull ache is manageable as long as I do not move them.

I'm surprised when she takes my hand, squeezing it gently. "Thank you for rescuing me. I'm so sorry you got hurt saving me."

I squeeze her hand in return, dipping my chin in acknowledgement, as her gaze holds mine.

Rolling thunder booms overhead as dark, ominous clouds spread out across the sky.

We must find shelter. My ship is not far from here. Even without the use of my wings, we should be able to reach it before nightfall.

I point to the mountain in the distance.

"Is that where you're from? Is that where we need to go?"

I nod.

She looks down at her feet. "I'm not sure how far I'll get in these."

My gaze drops to her tattered, slip-on shoes, and I understand her concern. I'm worried her feet will freeze before we even reach the shelter of the ship.

She sighs. "I wanted to steal some better shoes before I escaped, but I didn't have a chance. I just—" Her voice catches. "We had to take our chance when it came. We ran and didn't look back."

We. She said *we*, but I did not see her with anyone when I found her.

She stares off in the distance with a faraway look. Whoever her companion was, they must not have made it.

My heart breaks at her haunted expression. Cautiously, I wrap my arm around her shoulder and tug her to my side, wishing I could offer her comfort in her sadness.

It is strange how protective I feel of her... possessive even. I have only just met her, but it is as if something inside me is drawn to her. I feel as if she is mine... my mate. I have heard this happens among those who have the fated bond between them. I glance back at my wings, half expecting them to be glowing—indicating the presence of the bond—but they do not.

Still... I cannot help but wonder if she is my Al'essa—my Fated One. If she is, this would explain why I feel this way toward her.

I'm surprised when she hugs me in return, leaning into me. A low trilling hum thrums in my chest as I comfort her.

She sniffs, wipes her face and steps back, looking up at me with an expression I cannot quite discern. "Were you purring?"

A smile quirks my lips. It is actually known as 'trilling,' but purring is close enough. I nod.

She tips her head to the side, considering. "I like it. It sounds beautiful."

If she likes my trill, I will make use of it often.

I notice she still cradles her arm to her chest, and I'm sure it must pain her terribly. I should be able to heal it, however, once we reach my ship.

"All right." She tips up her chin. "Let's get moving. I'll just have to walk in these and make the best of it."

She starts to walk, but I grip her forearm to stop her. From my limited knowledge of her species, I understand that while the colder temperature may be good for dulling the pain from my injured wings, it is bad for her delicate Terran skin. Her people are unable to regulate their body temperatures as effectively as mine.

I point to her feet and then extend my arms. "Please. Allow me to carry you."

Having spent so much time with Alana—Vorek's Terran mate—I half expect her to protest, even though she can't understand my question. From my interactions with both Alana and Harry, I wonder if stubbornness is a trait of their species.

"Are you offering to carry me?"

I nod.

She gives me a hesitant look. "You're hurt too. You shouldn't have to carry me, Al'iro. It's all right. I can walk."

Does she not realize how slight her weight is? It is no burden to carry her at all.

A Lycaon howls in the distance; the sound echoing through the forest. Her eyes snap up to mine, wide with fear.

"It's one of those wolf guys from earlier, right?"

I nod.

A chorus of howls respond to the first one. I have heard this before when they track their prey. I suspect they are still chasing after the A'kai. We need to get to my ship before the A'kai find us.

We do not have time for her to walk when I am able to move much faster. The sooner we reach the safety of my ship, the better.

She lets out a surprised noise as I place one hand under her back and another behind her knees, and lift her to my chest.

She opens her mouth as if to protest, but quickly snaps it shut as another series of howls fills the woods again.

Without hesitating, I make my way to the mountain; the muscles along my back ache as the tendons throb along my wings, but, at least, it is bearable, unlike before. My nostrils flare at the scent of my own blood. Although the bleeding has stopped, I worry it might attract other predators to us.

I gaze out across the icy landscape and the snow-covered trees. The sun sinks low on the horizon. We only have an hour or less before nightfall, and we need to get to the ship before then. The A'kai and Lycaons are not the only creatures that hunt across the ice and snow.

Fierce protectiveness fills me as I carry Violet in my arms. The need to protect her is so intense it is almost overwhelming. It calls forth my primitive instincts and my desire to keep her close.

With each passing moment, my conviction only deepens. She is my Al'essa. Of this, I am certain. She must be my Fated One, for I can already sense emotions that are not mine—emotions I understand are coming from her.

I'd heard Fated mates could sense each other's emotions

even before sealing the bond, but I never imagined it would feel this strong. Nor did I realize it could happen so quickly.

Her fear travels along our bond like a tangible thing that twists around my heart.

I glance back at my wings, but do not find them glowing as they would if she were my fated one—my Al'essa. Perhaps they do not glow because they are injured.

Either way, it matters not because, as I glance down at her face, it is as if my soul recognizes hers. She is mine just as much as the heart that beats solidly within my chest. She is the part of me that I did not know was even missing.

For so long, after we became stranded here, I thought the Creator had abandoned me. Left me to waste away my days in this ice world of a planet. I was angry and, for a time, I even turned away on my beliefs.

But as I stare down at Violet, everything comes into sparkling clarity. I was never abandoned, as I'd believed. I was placed here so that my path might cross with hers. I am not cursed. I am blessed with something that many hope for but never receive.

This knowledge settles deep in my chest, and for the first time in forever, my heart feels lighter than it has in so many cycles.

This Terran female is mine. Mine to protect. Mine to cherish. Mine to love. And I will die before I allow any harm to come to her.

CHAPTER 3

AL'IRO

The thick canopy of trees overhead blocks the waning light from the sun. Only small slivers of illumination find their way through, casting the area around us in sinister glowing, orange-red hues as it filters through the red, needle-like leaves.

The howling grows distant behind us, and I pray the A'kai are still far enough away that they will not find us before we reach the ship.

Violet trembles slightly in my arms. Whether from fear or the cold, I am not sure, but I cradle her close to my body, wanting to give her comfort and warmth. She presses her hands and face to my chest, and I am in awe of the amount of trust she has in me not to harm her.

I wonder if she senses the bond as I do?

If she does, she has given no indication, but maybe the manifestation of it, for her, is the way she understands that I will not harm her... this trust she seems to already have in me.

When we reach the base of the mountain, her mouth drifts open as she stares up at the sheer cliff wall overhead. Her gaze darts briefly to my wings.

"How are we going to scale that?" she asks incredulously, pointing toward the cliff face wall. "It's almost straight up."

Gently, I set her feet on the ground. I lift my hand and slowly allow my dark claws to extend into sharp talons as she observes.

She lifts her own hands, showing me her blunt and useless nails. "There's no way I can climb that."

Again, I marvel at how her people have managed to survive as a species. Terrans lack claws, fangs, venom, wings... any form of natural defenses. It is a testament of their inner strength that they were able to survive being enslaved by the A'kai. Acid burns in my stomach at the thought of all the abuse she must have endured at their hands.

"You're going to have to leave me behind," she says.

I give her an incredulous look. I would never do this. Even if she were not my Al'essa, I would never think of leaving her to an uncertain fate. I extend my arms out to her. "Come. I will carry you."

Despite that she cannot understand my words, trustingly, she steps into the circle of my arms. She stretches up on her toes and wraps her arms around my neck and her legs around my waist.

As we scale up the cliff wall, she holds tightly to me. Her weight is so slight it would be concerning were I not already somewhat familiar with Terran anatomy. This is simply how her people are built. Vorek's Terran mate, Alana, is the same. Even Harry does not weigh much, despite being larger than the other Terrans we've encountered thus far.

I shift to one side, avoiding a jutting boulder in the rock face, and Violet winces slightly. Her arm injury must be more painful than she has indicated. The wound appears severe, but she has not complained.

This tells me she is strong. I suppose I should expect no less. Despite their smaller size, her people possess a strength of will and determination equal to that of mine.

Another small hiss of pain in my ear makes my heart clench. The wind catches her hair, lifting it away from her neck and filling my nostrils with her delicate scent. It reminds me of the *il'nora* flowers on my home world.

She squeezes her eyes shut, probably afraid to look as we ascend high above the ground.

"It's so strange. I can't believe that guy was a real were-wolf," she murmurs to herself, and I realize she is referring to the Lycaon. "Then again, you look just like some sort of handsome Fae prince from a fairy tale story."

My ears perk up. This is not the first time she has commented that she finds me handsome. My chest swells with pride. I am nothing special among my people. In fact, most females prefer a male with green or blue skin, believing these markings more beautiful because of their vibrancy. Purple is considered a rather dull color in comparison.

"You were really brave standing up to that wolf. I was so sure he was going to eat us." She pauses, a thoughtful expression on her face despite that her eyes are still closed. "That's the kind of story you can tell your children later on, you know? How you faced down a terrifying werewolf, looked him straight in the eye, unflinching, and made him back down."

My lips quirk in amusement as she speaks with a hint of awe and wonder in her tone.

"Yeah, definitely one to tell your family about," she muses.

She said she rambles—as she calls it—when she is nervous. I hate that she is afraid. I would never allow her to fall, but I cannot tell her this. Not in a way that she would understand me right now, at least.

Her brows draw together. "Are you married? Is there a Mrs. Al'iro at home?"

I shake my head, but her eyes are still shut, so she cannot see me. I feel it is important, however, that she knows I am unmated, especially with how I feel about her.

Gently, I touch her chin, tipping her face up to me. She carefully opens her eyes. I'm struck by how they seem to change colors from green to golden-brown based on the reflection of the light. I make a mental note to ask her about this strange, yet lovely, color variation when we reach the ship.

I shake my head in answer to her question and her cheeks go from pink to red.

I cannot help the smile that lights my face. I point to her, wanting to know if she is mated.

Slowly, she shakes her head. "No. I—I never got around to really dating anyone seriously, you know."

I want to roar my happiness to the stars that she is unmated. Instead, I nod and then force myself to focus on reaching the ship. Once we get there, I can heal her arm and fit her with another translator.

"You're an Aerilon, right?"

I nod.

"I heard your people were against slavery."

I nod again.

"Good," she says. A tear slips down her cheek, but she quickly brushes it away. "Sorry," she whispers. "I'm just still —" Her breath hitches. "I just lost my friend."

Despite that she cannot understand me, I whisper, "I am sorry."

She lifts her gaze to me. "If that's an 'I'm sorry'... then, thank you."

I nod, and she forces a pained smile to her lips.

As soon as we reach the plateau, I gently set her down on her feet, surprised by how much I miss the feel of her against me when she steps away.

Her eyes scan the forest below us as she cradles her injured arm to her chest. I'm struck again by how strong she is. I've seen patients with injuries not as severe as this who cried out as though they were dying. Yet, she simply grits her teeth and bears the pain without complaint.

I am eager to get inside the ship so I may treat her arm. It is cloaked so well I would probably never be able to locate it if I did not already know it was here. I extend my arm, waving my hand back and forth to search for the entrance. When I tap against something solid, I release a sigh of relief.

Violet watches curiously as I slide my hand along where I remember the door should be until I find the small indentation of the access panel off to the side. I press my palm flat against it, waiting for the computer to respond.

A low buzzing hum emits from the panel and a soft light appears, outlining the doors a moment before they slowly slide open.

Together, we step inside.

CHAPTER 4

VIOLET

As soon as we step inside, the doors seal shut behind us. Al'iro turns and taps a code into the panel next to the door. The display turns from red to solid green.

Bright lights flicker a moment and then turn on. My jaw drops as I study the interior. "This is a ship," I murmur more to myself than to him. "Did you crash here too?"

He nods.

"How did—" I start to ask more about it, but realize this is going to be a long conversation consisting mostly of hand gestures to get my point across.

He points to the wound on my arm, and motions for me to follow him.

All right. Questions can wait for later.

As we walk through the ship, I note the elegant trim and crown moldings carved in intricate nature designs that line the corridors and rooms. Soft glowing light filters down from the panels above. Thick plush brown carpet covers the floors, and the walls are a comforting shade of light green.

In several areas, flowering vines spill over from the containers above to drape down the walls in fascinating curtains of bioluminescent purples, reds, blues, and greens.

Al'iro leads me down a long hallway. I'm surprised by how beautifully decorated the interior is. This ship feels almost like a home.

I'm so fascinated by the design, I almost run into Al'iro's back when he stops in front of a set of doors.

He presses a panel beside them and they open into another brightly lit room. Sterile walls with sparkling glass panels and several medical beds tell me this must be the med bay. He guides me to one of the beds.

It's so tall that when I try to pull myself up onto it, I forget for a moment about my injured arm, and I gasp as pain shoots across my wound.

His warm hands wrap around my waist, helping me up. When I turn to him, he gives me an apologetic look and says something that I'm fairly sure is along the lines of "I'm sorry."

"It's all right," I tell him. "I forgot for a moment."

He gestures for me to lie down, so I do.

Something drops down from overhead, completely covering me and sealing me in some sort of box.

My heart begins hammering as the container snaps shut. I hate small, enclosed spaces. Dark memories of my time spent in cages flood my mind, and I beat on the glass, desperate to escape. Tears spring to my eyes, streaming down my face as I trace hands along the seams, trying to pry the casing open.

Al'iro's eyes widen, and his hands fly over a panel, tapping a screen.

The casing snaps open with a sharp hiss of air. He pulls the top away, and I try to jump off the bed, but he catches me mid-air.

My arms and legs flail widely a moment before I start pounding my fists against his chest, struggling to break free. I was wrong. He's not some knight-in-shining armor. He's trying to cage me. Just like the A'kai.

CHAPTER 5

AL'IRO

Violet beats her fists against me, the scent of her fear filling the air so thick, I taste it on my tongue. I release her immediately, and she races across the room to the doors, but they won't open. They're not coded to her yet.

She curls her hands into fists at her side and turns to face me. Despite the slight trembling of her body, she meets my gaze evenly. "I won't be caged again. Not by you or anyone."

Her fear tears at my heart so intense, I feel as if it will break. I hold up my hands in a placating gesture. "Please," I speak aloud, cursing myself for not trying to explain things to her first before I tried to heal her.

Despite that she cannot understand me, I try to explain myself, wanting only to remove the terror from her eyes. "I was not trying to put you in a cage. It's a Med Repair Unit (MRU). We use them to heal injuries. It can fit you with a new translator as well." I gesture behind my ear for emphasis, and then point to my mouth as I speak, hoping she understands.

She studies me warily.

Cautiously, I move closer. Most of the technology on the ship still works, but it is not reliable. The power cells were damaged during the crash and only remain on for short periods at a time before they must recharge. I probably have just enough time to get her in the MRU and heal her injuries, and fit her with a translator before most of the ship powers down.

I give her a pleading look and point to the MRU again before tapping behind my ear and then pointing again to my mouth.

Her small brow furrows. "Are you saying that thing can give me another translator?"

I nod.

She studies it a moment. A tear slips down her cheek, but she quickly brushes it away and tips up her chin. Her fear is still strong across the bond. "Fine. We need to be able to talk."

Bravely, she marches toward me, and I am surprised again by her strength of will and the amount of trust she places in me.

I turn back to the panel to activate it when the display goes dark. The overhead lights flicker off a moment before the emergency ones flick on.

With a heavy sigh of frustration, I lower my head. It seems the power cells are even worse off than they were the last time I was here. At least back then, everything stayed on for a few hours before shutting down again.

"What's wrong?" she asks.

I run a hand roughly through my hair, trying to decide the best way to tell her that I'm going to have to manually put her translator in her ear. I'm also going to have to search the ship for an emergency pack with healing gel, praying to the Creator that one may have been left behind so I can heal her injury because the MRU does not have enough power to run.

Ever so gently, I take her hand and meet her eyes evenly.

Her gaze holds mine, a wary expression on her face, but I notice she does not pull away.

Slowly, because I don't want to startle her, I run a scanner over her form. She remains still as I study the read out before me.

Rage floods my system when I notice the same marking on her back as the other Terrans we have found. The A'kai glyphs are jagged scars across her flesh that spell out the words *blood breeders*.

When I first saw this on Alana's back, I remember how horrified Vorek and I were as I scanned his mate's injuries. The A'kai are monsters. They want the Terrans not only for their blood, as a food source, but also for breeding.

Raw anger moves through me as I take note of the many wounds and fractures, identified on the scan, that are in various states of healing. Determination fills me. Vorek is right. We have to kill the A'kai. While they live, the Terrans will never be safe on this world.

I frown when I notice the same tracking device embedded in the back of her neck that the others had as well. I have no way to remove it now. I will have to try tomorrow when the MRU is working again.

In the meantime… I touch the spot behind her ear where her translator should be, then I point to the injector on the table beside us.

After a moment, she nods in understanding.

I ready the injector and then place it behind her ear. I'm about to depress the button when she wraps her hand around my wrist. "Wait!"

I still.

"I just need a moment to steady my nerves. It was really painful when the slavers fitted me with a translator."

My heart clenches. The ones who gave her the first translator must not have used an anesthetic to dull the pain. I cannot even begin to imagine how terrible that must have been for her. I would never do this to anyone. There is a small amount of anesthetic in the injector, but I have no way to tell her this.

She draws in a deep breath and takes my free hand with her own. "All right. I'm ready."

Violet squeezes her eyes shut, and when I press the injector, she immediately goes limp in my arms.

Panic wraps tight around my spine. "Violet?"

She doesn't respond. Quickly, I lay her down and then run a scanner over her, frantically studying the read out on the display.

Everything appears normal, but I cannot be certain. I've only ever treated Alana and Harry. I know that some species are known to fall unconscious after receiving the translator chip, but I do not remember Alana or Harry discussing this about theirs.

I brush the hair back from her face, desperate as I watch her eyes, praying that her eyelids will flutter and open. Pain stabs through my chest, and myriad thoughts run through my mind of what may have happened—none of them good.

What if I hurt her? What if I somehow damaged her brain?

I cup her face and brush the soft pad of my thumb over her cheek as I struggle to contain my worries and fears.

She trusted me. She trusted me, and I hurt her. I will never forgive myself.

Panicked, I scan her again. If my readings are correct, she should wake up soon. If I'm wrong, she might never recover from whatever damage I've done to her.

She shivers slightly. She appears so vulnerable, it tears at my heart.

I gather her in my arms, needing to hold her close. Raw pain and anguish fill me as I carry her limp form down the hallway, to what used to be my quarters.

Everything is just as I left it; nothing has been disturbed. The floating bed in the corner with the deep purple comforter and several white furs I've added as well. The desk and chair across the way with my tablet right where I placed it last time I was here.

Gently, I lay her beneath the blankets on the bed, tucking the comforter and furs around her to keep her warm. I pull the chair up next to her so I may keep watch, wanting to make sure I do not miss anything if she needs me.

She lies with a stillness that worries me.

I tap the control console next to the bed, activating the perimeter alarm. If the A'kai are somehow able to receive a signal from her tracker in here, we will be alerted immediately if they approach.

Leaning forward in my chair, I study her closely. I will never forgive myself if I have harmed her. Now, I must wait and pray that she is unharmed. I send a silent prayer to the Creator, begging for my Al'essa to awaken soon.

CHAPTER 6

VIOLET

When I open my eyes, I find golden ones staring down at me in concern. "Are you all right?" Al'iro asks, and I note the panic in his voice. "Can you understand me?"

"Yes." I exhale a long sigh of relief. "Thank you. That didn't hurt at all."

He blinks several times, and I watch as his shoulders sag forward. "Thank the Creator," he murmurs under his breath.

I sit up, glancing in confusion at my surroundings. The last thing I remember was being in the Med Bay. "What happened? Where are we?"

"You fell unconscious after I injected the translator chip. I brought you to my quarters here on the ship. You slept through the night."

I notice the dark rings under his eyes. "What about you? Did you... get any sleep?"

He shakes his head. "I could not."

"Why?"

"I was... concerned for you." Before I can respond, he glances down at my injured arm. "Was this from blaster fire?"

I nod, swallowing against the lump in my throat as memories of Elain resurface. "The A'kai killed my friend," I barely manage. A tear slips down my cheek, but I quickly brush it away.

His expression is full of pain as he studies me. "I am sorry."

Dark memories fill my mind and I close my eyes briefly against the raw pain that stabs at my heart. "The two of us... we were trying to escape."

He takes my hand and gives me a pitying look. "You are safe now," he says. "I have activated the perimeter alarm to alert us of anyone outside the ship."

He looks down at my injured arm. "I am a Healer. We need to get this cleaned up and bandaged. I wanted to use the MRU to do this, but the power cells are charging on the cruiser. They were damaged in the crash and only remain on for a short period of time during the day. It will take them a few more hours before they are ready."

Panic tightens my chest. "Are you talking about that box you put me in?"

"Forgive me," he offers. "It was not my intention to scare you."

I nod. My gaze drifts to his back. "What about your wings?"

"I can try healing them as soon as the power cells are charged and everything is working again."

I dart a glance around the room. "So... you crashed here too?"

"Yes. Five cycles ago."

I start to ask more questions, but stop as I observe him.

He reaches into a drawer and pulls out a few bandages and a bottle of liquid that smells like some sort of antiseptic.

His golden eyes meet mine. "Please, allow me to clean your wound. I need to bandage it."

"All right."

I hold my arm out to him, noting how gently he takes it. How long has it been since someone cared for me like this? "This will sting a bit," he cautions, holding up the antiseptic.

Gritting my teeth, I brace myself. When he pours it over my wound, the pain flares brightly, but I force myself to remain still to allow him to work.

As he carefully wraps my arm, he continues talking. "We can try to contact my people when the computers are back up. I tried when we first got here, but the signal would not go through. Probably because of the storm."

"I thought *this* was your ship."

"It is," he replies.

"Then... where are your people?"

"When we crashed on this planet, it damaged our power cells. They take hours to recharge. As a result, only a few of the systems still work, and then... not for very long. We abandoned it when we allied ourselves with the V'loryns and moved to their territory."

"V'loryns," I murmur, more to myself than to him. "That's what the slavers all thought I was, before the A'kai bought me. I heard from an Aerilon slave that V'loryns, Aerilon, and Mosaurans were good. That all three of your species were anti-slavery."

"That is correct," he replies.

"What about those wolves?" I shudder inwardly, recalling the werewolf guy. "Do you think they're hunting us?"

He frowns. "Wolves?"

"The men that shifted into animals."

"Ah," he says. "Yes, they are called Lycaons. And... I do not think so. I used to believe they were bad, but now, I am not

43

so sure. He told us he would buy us time to run while he fought off the A'kai."

"He was helping us?" I ask incredulously. "I thought for sure he wanted to eat you."

A smile quirks my lips, and I arch a brow. "He seemed genuinely offended when you voiced as much aloud. It was… surprising. I always thought they were hostile and uncommonly aggressive. I did not realize they possessed such a strong sense of honor as well."

"So… why do you think he helped us?"

"The A'kai are a common enemy."

"The enemy of my enemy is my friend," I murmur.

He arches a questioning brow.

"It's an old saying on my world."

"And a wise one, it seems," he adds. "Particularly as things stand between us now."

"What do you mean?"

"We were one of five ships that crashed on this ice world five cycles ago. Us, the V'loryns, Mosauran, Lycaons and A'kai. Our vessels were pulled into a wormhole while we were fighting amongst each other over a border dispute."

"That's what happened to us," I offer. "The A'kai slave ship was pulled into a wormhole. It damaged the engines, so we had to leave on the escape pods." I frown. "Are you telling me there were already more A'kai on this world before we even arrived?"

"Yes." He clenches his jaw. "And with the arrival of the escape pods from the ship you were on, their numbers have now grown."

"So you're stranded on this world too?"

He nods. "All of us are."

I allow my gaze to travel over the room. "Are we safe in here?"

"Yes. There should be enough power to keep the cloak working to conceal the ship."

Relief fills me as I recall what it looked like when we first arrived. The ship was so well hidden, I wouldn't have even guessed it was here before he opened the doors to let us in.

"What were you doing out there?" I ask. "When you rescued me?"

"I was searching for your people."

"You were looking for Terrans? Why?"

"We saw the escape pods fall from the sky not long ago. We found two of your people; they have been taken in by mine and the V'loryns. Another two by the Mosaurans."

Hope fills me. "Who did you find?"

"Alana and Harry are the two with us. Lara and Emma are with the Mosaurans."

"They're all right?"

"Yes."

"How come everyone is spread out? Why aren't Lara and Emma with your people as well?"

"The Mosaurans have their own territory not far from ours."

"But they're allies of yours? Like the V'loryns?"

"Yes, Vorek is the V'loryn commander, but I also consider him a close and personal friend. He and I were both captured and forced to fight in the gladiator rings together before we were rescued. He is the one who is mated to Alana."

"Mated? You mean… married?" I ask incredulously.

He nods.

"My friend is married to an alien?" The words escape my lips unfiltered, so I quickly apologize. "I'm sorry. I didn't mean—"

"It is all right."

"It's just that… before I was taken, my people had never

even been outside of our planetary system, much less met any other species."

"Lara is mated to Commander Markus as well."

"Is he V'loryn too?"

He shakes his head. "No, he is Mosauran. Lara was his fated one. Just as Alana was to Vorek."

"Fated one?"

"Destined by the Creator," he explains. "Alana told me it was akin to soul mates according to your culture."

I used to believe in fate and soul mates, but that was before everything that happened. Now… I don't know what I believe anymore.

A sudden thought occurs to me and a chill shivers down my spine.

Is this why they are searching for us? Because they want women?

"Is that the price?"

He frowns. "The… price?"

Dark memories flood my mind, and I fist my hands at my sides, squeezing my eyes shut against the pain. The A'kai never physically raped me, but they violated my mind several times in the *R'ugol*—the forced mind link. I used to try to tell myself that—at least they had not yet violated my body, as well… but now, it seems I might not avoid that fate after all.

I force my gaze to his. "If the price of my freedom is my body, I refuse to pay it," I grind out.

His head jerks back. "My people… we would never force ourselves upon a female. I swear it to the Creator of all things."

The expression on his face is nothing short of wounded. "On my honor as a soldier, I would never touch you against your will, Violet."

As I study him, something deep inside me tells me I can trust him, and he's telling me the truth.

"I believe you," I murmur. "If you meant me harm, you could have already done it by now."

"I would sooner end my own life than ever harm you, Violet."

"I'm sorry." I lower my gaze. "I've just been through so much. It's hard to trust people."

The lights flicker off and then back on again. Worry fills me. "What's going on?"

"The power cells are still charging, so we only have emergency lighting and basic systems. While they are recovering, we need to locate an emergency med kit. I need healing gel to treat your arm."

Worry fills me. His nostrils flare. "I can scent your fear, Violet. I promise I will not harm you."

"I'm not afraid of you," I reply quickly because it's true. "I'm worried about the A'kai. What will happen if the power cells go out? Will the cloak stop working?"

"No. It is on an independent system."

"What about the heat?" I ask.

A shiver runs through me as I remember the storm that was coming and how cold it was outside. It's a bit chilly in here, but nothing compared to out there.

He studies me in concern. "Are you cold?"

"Just a bit."

He grabs another fur at the foot of the bed and drapes it over my shoulders. "Come. We will find you some warmer clothing."

CHAPTER 7

VIOLET

The emergency lighting flickers softly as we make our way through the ship, casting an eerie glow throughout the space. We pass by several large open rooms and a few spaces along the wall that look as though they've been stripped bare. Wires dangle free from missing panels along the walls and ceiling in several places.

As if sensing my gaze upon them, he explains. "We have stripped several items from our ship to retrofit them to the V'loryn's cruiser."

"The V'loryns' have a working ship?"

"Yes. We live in it. The systems all work, thanks in part to the items we've taken from our vessel, but the engines do not. They were damaged in the crash." He pauses. "Still... it is nice to have working technology on this barren planet."

"It sounds nice," I agree.

We continue on. He stops at various locations, sifting through drawers and panels in the wall, searching for an emergency med kit.

When he comes up empty after the third one, he sighs. "I fear we may have removed them all and taken them to the V'loryn ship. There is one more place we might find one."

He circles back down the long hallway lined with several doors that we were in earlier. As soon as he opens the first one, I recognize this must have been the crew's quarters.

I note that some have been stripped of almost all their belongings: furniture, blankets, decorations. While others appear relatively undisturbed. As if their occupants might return at any moment. Sadness fills me when I realize these must belong to the ones who didn't make it.

Al'iro moves to a nearby desk. He pulls open a drawer and then stills. "Did you find one?" I ask from across the room.

He shakes his head.

I move to his side and find him staring at a picture on a tablet. Several Aerilon dressed in what I assume are military uniforms stand side by side. "Were they your crew?"

"No," he says, his voice low. "This was my sister's graduating class from the Academy." He darts a glance around the room. "This must have been Il'ura's quarters. They graduated together. She was good friends with my sister—En'lora."

I study the image. "Which one is your sister?"

He points to an Aerilon woman near the center. She looks so much like him, I smile. "You two could pass for twins."

"Yes," he murmurs. "Many people used to remark upon this."

He points to another Aerilon man. "This was my best friend—Al'aneo. We all grew up together," he adds. A wistful smile curves his lips. "She had feelings for him, but whenever I would ask her, she'd always deny it."

"Are they both back on the V'loryn ship?"

With a slight clench of his jaw, he lowers his head.

"Al'aneo is a captain of his own ship. And my sister... she died seven cycles ago."

"What happened to her?" Inwardly, I curse myself when I realize I've asked this aloud.

"All three of us served on the same ship. Al'aneo was captain. She was captured by the A'kai while on a dangerous mission."

I inhale sharply.

He continues. "We rescued her, but... En'lora took her own life on the way back to Aerilon. She could not live with the nightmares of what had happened to her."

My mouth drifts open. "I'm so sorry."

He pockets the picture. "Thank you." He changes the subject. "What about you? Do you have any family?"

I shake my head. "Elain—my friend that was—" I stop short, not wanting to say 'killed.' After a moment, I continue. "She was with me right before you rescued me... she was like a sister to me."

Tears sting my eyes and despite my attempt to blink them back, the first one escapes my lashes and rolls down my cheek. "She got hit by blaster fire. She told me to go on..." I look down at my hands. "I left her, Al'iro." A broken sob escapes me. "She told me to leave her... and I did, but I shouldn't have."

He carefully wraps an arm around my shoulder and pulls me to his chest. Another sob escapes me as tears stream down my cheek.

"Your friend was very brave," he whispers. "She wanted you to live."

"How could I just leave her like that? I should have stayed. I should have—"

"If you had stayed, you both would have died," he whispers. "You honor her memory, by living." His golden eyes meet mine. "Do you understand? You cannot give up. She would not want you to. Would you not have done the same for her?"

Reluctantly, I nod. He's right. I would have. But it still doesn't make it any easier right now.

"I am sorry, Violet," he whispers softly. "I wish I had found you both sooner."

Something about his words breaks me and more tears begin to fall. He holds me close as I cry for Elain and for all the others that are still out there.

I'm not sure how long we remain like this, but he doesn't speak or complain. He merely holds me, smoothing a hand across my back and shoulders as I let out all my pain.

"You are safe now," he murmurs softly above me. I'm not sure why, but I trust him when he says this. I'm not one who easily trusts. Especially, after all that I've been through. But something deep inside me tells me that I can trust him.

The old me—before I was taken—would have trusted this feeling immediately. But the new me—the one that experienced life in a cage—worries that I'm trusting too quickly. That maybe my trauma is making me reach out for the first person who wants to take care of me.

Even so... I can't ignore the feeling in my heart.

After what feels like forever, I finally stop.

Silence stretches out between us a moment before he looks to me. "I am sorry you have been through so much."

Unable to speak through my emotions, I nod.

After a moment, he looks to me. "We must continue searching for an emergency med kit and healing gel for your wound."

I follow behind him as he searches various compartments, each of them turning up nothing.

Finally, he turns to me, his golden eyes filled with sadness. "Forgive me, but I do not believe we will find an emergency med kit here. I am sorry. We must have moved them all to the other ship."

"That's all right." I hold up my arm. "At least it's bandaged. So, it's fine for now."

He gives me a pained look.

"What's wrong?"

He looks down at his hands. "I am sorry."

"For what?"

"I am a Healer. I am sorry that the best I can offer you is bandages. You must be in pain and I—"

I touch his arm, drawing his attention back to me. "It's all right." I give him a warm smile. "You rescued me. I would be dead right now, if not for you." I gesture to his wings. "I'm the one who should be apologizing to you. I'm the reason your wings are injured."

"I could not let you die," he says. "Not when there was something I could do."

"Thank you," I whisper. "For rescuing me. After everything I've been through, I never expected to find kindness in this part of the universe."

"You are most welcome."

We talk a while longer while he continues searching the ship for more supplies. It seems a lot of things have been completely picked clean, but he manages to find some food and some more clothing for me.

After a while he turns to me. His brow furrows softly. "I have a question."

"What is it?"

"You said something yesterday, and I did not understand what it meant. "You said I was a 'knight-in-shining armor.'"

A smile tugs at my mouth, and I decide to tease him. "Well, it doesn't matter anymore, because I take it back."

"Why?" He frowns. "What does it mean?"

"Basically, a gentleman who saves someone." I arch a

brow. "Not a man who lets someone ramble on about how handsome she thinks he is without telling her that he knows exactly what she's saying."

He barks out a laugh. "Can you blame me? What male does not want to hear that he is handsome?"

I roll my eyes. "I take it back."

He laughs again. "I will still know it is true, regardless." He tips up his chin. "When we return to my people, they will be jealous that such a beautiful female finds me attractive. Because of my dull coloring, I have never been one sought after. They will be puzzled if nothing else."

"Dull coloring?"

"My purple skin tone. It is… considered dull compared to the vibrant blues and greens of most males."

My gaze travels over his form. From his heavily muscled body, layered with thick cords of muscle to his perfect, full lips. "You're the most handsome man I've ever seen."

He flashes a gorgeous smile. "Be sure to tell that to everyone when we see them."

I laugh. "Don't worry, I've got you covered."

He laughs again.

CHAPTER 8

VIOLET

It's been several hours that we've been waiting for the power cells to charge enough to try the MRU. By the time they're ready, he leads me back to the Med Bay.

He turns to me. "I'm going to try to remove your tracker first. Then, if there is enough power, I will see if it can repair my wings."

"No," I counter. "You should fix your wings first. If you can fly us out of here, we'll be safer. Then, when we reach your people, you can remove my tracker there."

He hesitates a moment before nodding. "I understand what you are suggesting, but it goes against my instincts to not treat you first, Violet."

I take his hand. "And that's why I like you."

His eyes snap up to mine, and a slow smile curves his mouth.

I continue. "But I think it would be better to see if we can fix you first, all right?"

He nods.

He shows me how to activate the panel and then lies down in the MRU. It closes over him, and my heart clenches as I watch it seal him in. I glance at him through the glass and then gently place my hand on top, wanting to offer him comfort.

I know he's not scared, but I am scared for him. Even the thought of him in this small, enclosed space makes my stomach twist in a knot.

My heart clenches as Al'iro places his palm on the glass beneath mine and flashes a devastatingly handsome smile, as if trying to reassure me he's all right.

He's so caring and thoughtful. My heart flutters in my chest. I can't believe he's considered 'dull' on his world. He's the most gorgeous man I've ever seen.

I press the button, like he showed me, and the panel lights up as the MRU scans him.

I may not be a doctor, but from what I can see, his wings are broken. Badly. I shudder inwardly. He has to be in a lot of pain, but he hides it well.

As it scans him, a flashing red symbol appears on the screen. His mouth drifts open as he studies it before he gives me the signal to open the MRU casing.

I press the panel again, and the casing unsnaps and lifts away. He sits up and sighs heavily. "The damage is… more extensive than I believed. No wonder it does not hurt as much now. Many of the nerve endings were damaged. I will have to be treated back at the ship. It cannot be done here."

Sadness tightens my chest. "I'm so sorry. You're hurt because of me. I—"

"It is not your fault, Violet," he says. "Besides, I would not change anything even if given the chance again. It was worth it to save you."

He stands and gestures for me to lie down. "I should be able to heal your arm now, though," he says.

I stare at the box a moment and then cautiously lie down. "I hate small spaces," I tell him. "They remind me of the cages."

"I will be here with you." He takes my hand. "I promise I will work as quickly as I can."

"All right." I breathe in and out through pursed lips to calm myself as it closes over me.

He presses a button on the console and his warm, velvet voice comes over a speaker inside. "You are doing well, Violet. I am here with you."

I would say something back, but I can't. I'm too anxious to speak.

Without warning, the lights shut off and the emergency ones flick back on.

Panic sets in as I hear the machine wind down, and I'm terrified that I might be trapped.

"Get me out! Please!"

He quickly lifts away the casing. I jerk up to sitting, and he wraps his arms around me, smoothing a hand soothingly down my back in comfort as I struggle to calm my breathing. "I'm sorry," I whisper.

"It's all right," he says. "You're safe. I have you."

I pull back just enough to meet his gaze. His golden eyes search my own as I reach up and cup his cheek. I could so easily get lost in their depths.

Maybe it's foolish to trust someone so quickly, but I do. There's something about him that feels so familiar. I've heard that shared trauma can bond two people very quickly, and I think it must be true. Because the only other explanation for what I feel right now is something I thought was only a myth.

I've heard of people finding their soulmates and the instant knowing that comes with something like this. But I never thought it could actually be true.

I lean in, and he drops his forehead gently to mine. For the first time in a long time, I feel safe. And as his eyes stare deep into mine, I no longer feel so alone. It's as if my soul has found its other half.

My brain protests that I'm crazy, but my heart insists that I'm not. After everything I've been through, would it be wrong to just let go and trust that what I feel is something real?

The warmth of his breath fans across my skin. He smells like a combination of warm cinnamon and earth. My heart pounds in my chest as I slowly brush my lips against his in a tender kiss.

His lips are soft and warm.

In the back of my mind, I know that we've only just met, but it doesn't matter. This feels right, somehow, but I can't explain it. As if something deep inside my soul recognizes his.

Dark memories flood my mind, and I still. Although the A'kai never physically raped me, the things they did in my mind during the R'ugol still felt very real.

I place a hand on Al'iro's chest and carefully push away from him before standing.

"Violet," he says, his gaze searching mine in concern. "What is wrong?"

My eyes drop to his pants and the obvious bulge beneath his clothing. "I can't do this," I whisper. "I'm sorry."

He stands and gently cups my cheek. "You do not have to apologize," he says. "I would never take anything from you that you do not wish to give."

His words and his expression reassure me. "Thank you."

"There is something I must tell you," he says.

The way he says this gives me pause. Worry tightens my chest as I ask, "What is it?"

"My people believe in a fated bond. When we find our

fated mates, our wings begin to glow and we feel very protective and possessive of the one who is ours."

I blink several times. "Why are you telling me this?"

His gaze holds mine intently. "Because I believe you are my Fated One—my Al'essa."

I dart a glance at his wings. "But... your wings... they're not glowing."

"It matters not," he says. "I believe they do not glow because they are injured. But I am certain they will once they are healed."

"How do you know this?"

He takes my hand and brings it to his chest, directly over his heart. "Because I feel it here... in my heart." His golden eyes search mine. "Do you... feel anything between us as well?"

I could lie and say *no*, but I don't want to do this. Not to him. "Yes."

A faint smile curves his mouth. "What do you feel?"

My brow furrows as I try to think of how to explain. "Like I've known you forever. Like I'm... safe with you. Even though we've only just met. It's a knowing," I admit. "But I... can't explain it."

Warmth heats my cheeks as his gaze holds mine.

Gently, he touches my face. "This coloring... it is beautiful."

Embarrassed, I lower my gaze. "Thank you," I whisper.

He flashes a devastatingly handsome smile before his expression sobers. "I understand that your species does not have fated bonds. I have heard this from the others. So I want you to understand that I will not pressure you in any way. If you decide you do not wish me as your mate, I will accept it.

"In my culture, it is the female that chooses. I ask only that you allow me to care for and protect you."

"Al'iro, even though I feel something... I—" I pause, unsure how to continue. "I'm just not sure that I'll—"

"What is it?" he asks.

A tear slips down my cheek. "That I'll ever want to be touched like that."

He gently brushes away my tears as his gaze meets mine. "I ask only to be allowed to remain at your side. I want to protect you and help you in any way that I can." He takes both of my hands in his and drops to one knee. "Please, will you allow me to remain at your side so I may do this?"

As I look to him, I realize just how alone I am. Here he is offering to help me and protect me and asking nothing in return. I have to trust someone, especially if I'm going to survive in this strange new world I now find myself in. "Yes."

It's almost dark outside as Al'iro leads me down the hall and back to his room. It's strange. I would have thought that his confession would have made things awkward between us. Instead, it feels more comfortable in a way.

I know for certain he would never hurt me or try to take advantage of me. If anything, this makes me feel even more safe than I did before.

CHAPTER 9

AL'IRO

"What are we going to do now?" she asks as she walks beside me, back to my quarters.

My thoughts turn again to the memory of our kiss. If she were Aerilon, we would have already sealed our bond. The thought of holding her in my arms again fills my entire body with warmth.

My nostrils flare as I draw her scent deep into my lungs. Everything about her calls to my soul and I long to claim her. I desire more than anything to seal the bond between us, and take her up into the sky for the mating flight.

With a heavy sigh, I force myself to push these errant thoughts from my mind. Besides... she has been through much. She may not want any of this. And if she does not... I will accept it. I would never pressure her.

Even if she wanted me, my wings are injured, and they might never be repaired. We might never have a mating flight. The damage I read on the MRU readout was... extensive.

I turn to her. "We will try to remove your tracker as well as heal your arm again tomorrow, after the power cells have recharged."

"What if we can't?"

"I have not given up on trying to contact my people. Once the weather clears, I will try again to get a signal."

As we enter my quarters, her eyes sweep over the room. Her gaze drifts to the floating bed along the far wall, piled high with furs, where she woke up earlier. She looks to the table and chairs in front of the computer console and the sofa across the way. "It looks like you left everything here," she says, and I recognize the question in her statement.

"Not everything," I reply. "We return every few months to check that our distress signal is still transmitting as well as to salvage more supplies to take back to the other ship. I... prefer to sleep in my quarters while we are here those few days."

What is this?" Violet asks as she gestures to a door on the opposite wall.

"A cleansing room." I point out the sink and toilet, but when I show her the ion shower, she shrinks back. The acrid scent of her fear fills the air, and I frown. "What is wrong?"

Her gaze is locked on the shower, a faraway look on her face. "The masters used to put me under one of these. It was very painful," she whispers. "It felt like my skin was rubbed raw."

Choking anger rises from within me.

How could they use the highest setting on skin as fragile as hers?

I turn to her. "I believe they used one of the highest settings on you. It is not supposed to hurt, when used properly."

Numbly, she nods.

"I will program it to the lowest setting. It will not hurt you, Violet."

"Thank you," she says softly.

My heart swells with pride at her trust in me. In my culture, trust granted to a male from a female is one of the greatest honors imaginable. A female only declares her trust to the male she has chosen for her mate. That is why the mating flight is so sacred. The female trusts the male to fly them safely as they consummate their bonding.

I dip my chin in a firm bow. "You honor me with your trust, Violet."

Guiding her to the ion shower, I stand with her beneath it. I activate the lowest setting and allow it to pass over us. It finishes a moment later, and she blinks several times before glancing down at her body. "That-that didn't hurt. Not at all."

She smiles up at me, and I stare completely transfixed. She is the most beautiful female I have ever seen.

"Can you show me how to work this?"

Still staring at her, it takes me a moment to respond and form the words to reply, "Yes, I can."

After I'm finished showing her, we move back into the bedroom. I move to the closet to retrieve a few more furs I have stored here as well, wanting to make certain she is as warm as possible tonight.

When I lift them from the shelf, an emergency med kit bag tumbles from the pile onto the floor. I breathe out a sigh of relief, thanking the Creator for this boon. I'd forgotten that I left this here. "I found an emergency bag."

"Thank goodness," she answers.

I return to her side, and gesture for her to sit on the sofa as I pull out the med scanner. "Will you allow me to scan you? I need to assess your wound again before I heal it."

She nods, and I carefully remove her bandage. I move the

scanner over her forearm. The flesh burnt and swollen from the blaster hit. "We do not need to wait for the MRU. We can use the healing gel."

I rifle through the emergency med bag and hold the tube up to her. "I must apply this to your injury."

"You're sure it will work on me?"

"Yes. I have treated your kind with it before. But I must warn you… it is rather painful." I pause. "Once I apply it, you cannot touch it. You must allow it to work."

"Does it work fast?"

"Yes. It may make you fall asleep after we use it though."

She holds out her arm, and I don't miss the slight tremor of her hand as she does. She tips her chin up, clenching her jaw. "All right."

Once more, I'm surprised by her strength of character, as well as her complete and utter trust in me. I only hope I do not lose it when I treat her. Harry said the healing gel was one of the most painful experiences of his life.

I dab some onto my first two fingers, hovering over her injury as I ready to apply it. Her small hand on my opposite forearm stops me abruptly.

I flick my gaze up to her.

"Do you have something I can bite down on?"

I frown.

"For the pain."

I dart a glance around the room and notice a small pillow on the bed and hand it to her. Before she puts it in her mouth, her eyes—golden-brown in this moment—search mine. "All right. I'm ready."

She bites the pillow, and I carefully apply the gel to her injury. The moment it touches her skin, she releases a muffled cry of pain that stops my heart.

I'm shocked when her right hand grabs mine, squeezing

with a strength I did not realize her people possessed, her entire body tense with pain.

I hold her hand, watching in satisfaction as the tissue on her injured arm slowly reknits.

CHAPTER 10

VIOLET

Blinding pain sears my skin, nearly as painful as the original injury itself. Without thinking, I grip Al'iro's hand tightly as I try to remain still. Every instinct inside me screams for me to rub the gel off... anything to end the burning sensation traveling across my wound.

I squeeze my eyes shut, biting down on the pillow with a muffled cry as waves of pain move through me.

After what feels like an eternity, the sensation slowly begins to ebb. I glance down and see the skin is now completely healed. Relief washes over me, and my entire body relaxes. Slowly, I release my grip on Al'iro's hand and allow myself to fall back on the sofa.

Closing my eyes, I succumb to my exhaustion and drift away into oblivion.

When I open my eyes, I'm lying in a bed, tucked beneath a layer of soft, white fur. Panic wrests my heart, and I jerk up to sitting.

"You are safe, Violet," Al'iro's voice calls softly.

I turn to find him on the sofa. He stands and walks over to me, kneeling beside the bed. "Are you all right?"

"I just… forgot where I was for a moment." I glance around the space. "How long are we going to stay here?"

"A storm has moved in on us. We must shelter here until it passes." He runs a hand through his short, dark hair. "In the morning, after the power cells have had time to charge, I will try contacting my people again."

I start to ask more about this, but stop when I notice his wings still hanging limp behind him. I glance down at my forearm, the skin healed as if it were never injured in the first place. "Can the healing gel help your wings?"

I study the damaged areas, noting the deformed appearance of the clear, membranous structures. I may not be a doctor but I recognize a broken bone when I see one. "Will this mend the broken bones?"

"Not completely; it will set them as they are. It cannot straighten them on its own. But it will reknit the tissue to avoid infection and help with the pain a bit." He pauses. "Normally, my kind heal without use of the gel, but not our wings. When we return to my people, my wings will have to be rebroken and repaired by one of the other Healers."

Tears sting my eyes, but I blink them back. "I'm so sorry you were injured because of me."

"Do not apologize, my Al'essa. I would do it all again, if given the chance."

In his eyes, I see the truth. He would sacrifice himself for me. He already has… more than once.

Gently, I spread the gel across the areas of broken skin.

He grits his teeth through the pain I'm sure is searing like fire across his flesh.

I watch in awe as the torn tissue reknits before my eyes, as good as new. The deformed areas are still visible, but at least the skin is now closed. I almost don't want to ask, but I have to know. "Will you be able to fly again?"

He lowers his gaze. "In truth, I do not know. The injuries are… extensive, according to the MRU."

My heart clenches. "Is the pain any better, at least?" I ask, praying that he's not hurting anymore.

Slowly, I observe as he carefully flexes his wings to test them. "Yes, it feels much better."

He studies me a moment, a question behind his eyes. "Did you mean to—" he starts, but stops, considering his words before continuing. "When you jumped, you meant to end your life," he finally says, and I recognize his statement is also a question.

"I knew it was either death or enslavement again." Tears sting my eyes. "The things they did to us… I could not go back." I curl my hands into fists at my side as I meet his gaze evenly. "I will never be taken again."

His golden gaze holds mine a moment before speaking. "Know this: Even if you decide you do not want me as your mate, I wish only to remain at your side so that I may protect you and keep you safe. You are my Al'essa. I would give my life without hesitation to defend yours."

Emotions lodge in my throat, but I somehow manage to speak around them. "Thank you."

CHAPTER 11

AL'IRO

She blinks back her tears and clenches her jaw. In her eyes, I recognized the truth. She would truly rather die than be taken by the A'kai ever again. I understand this. I was a slave, too. But I never suffered under the hands of the A'kai. Not like my sister, En'lora.

I lost En'lora to the darkness. She never recovered from the trauma of her enslavement. She took her own life because of this.

As I gaze at Violet, I know I will do whatever it takes to make sure she does not succumb to the darkness as my sister did. I will guard her with my life. When we return to my people, I will speak with them. We must hunt down the A'kai as Vorek suggested. I will not risk them capturing my mate again.

"Do you think there are more of my people still alive?" she asks, pulling me back from my thoughts. "There were at least twenty of us... maybe more on the A'kai ship."

"We hope so," I tell her. "That is why we are still searching. Do you remember how you were taken in the first place?"

"No. I went into stasis sleep and woke up in a cage on a Zovian ship. They all thought I was V'loryn, but the A'kai... they somehow knew what I was." She pauses. "They want my people for their blood. They are searching for other Terrans and for our home world."

Ice fills my veins at the mere thought. If the A'kai ever find their world, I doubt her kind could stand against the might of their Empire. They would be conquered and enslaved.

"That's why they searched our minds so often. They thought we would lead them to Terra. But none of us know where it is. My people have never even been outside our planetary system. We knew nothing about other races out here in the universe." She pauses. "I was an engineer. I was so excited to go into space, but I realize now that I was so naïve. I always imagined making first contact with another species... that it would be peaceful—an exchange of friendship and ideas..." Her voice trails off. "I was so wrong."

Vorek's mate—Alana—has shared this with me, but I find it so strange to think that their people never left their system. Mine have been traveling the stars for thousands of years. "I am sorry," I whisper softly. "But please know not all races are hostile to others. You will be safe with my people. I promise."

"You think they'll accept me?"

"Of course," I reply quickly, wanting to assuage her concerns. "Everyone was glad for the addition of Alana and Harry, for we gained two new crew members."

"Crew members?"

"Yes. Harry goes out every day to help search for more of your people and Alana helps me in the Med Bay as a Healer."

Hope sparks in her eyes. "Do you have any need for another engineer?"

"There is always a need for engineers." I smile. "Especially if we want to continue living in the comfort we have now with the technology of the V'loryn ship."

As she continues to ask me questions about the ship and the rest of our crew, I am eager to get her back to our territory. Not only will she be safer there, but I am certain she will find her place among our people.

She is intelligent, brave, kind and beautiful; with a strength of will equal to that of my people. As we talk, I realize that, even without the fated bond between us, I would still desire her as mine.

"Thank you, Al'iro," she says, pulling me back from my thoughts.

"For what?"

She smiles and it is as bright as the sun. "For giving me hope again."

Happiness blooms in my chest. It is strange how much she already means to me, but I do not question it. Even if the bond is responsible for drawing me to her, I am thankful for it. She is everything I could ever want in another, and I will do anything to make sure she is happy and safe.

CHAPTER 12

VIOLET

He gestures to the panel beside the door. I place my palm on it, and he lays his hand over mine. The smell of warm cinnamon and earth fills the air around us and I drink in his scent. He stands so close behind me, the warmth of his body radiates to mine as he speaks softly in my ear. "Now, the ship is coded to recognize you. You may come and go anywhere as you please."

When he steps back, he opens the door as if to leave. "Where are you going?"

"I will be in the quarters right beside yours." He gestures to another door. "The cleansing room is through there if you need it."

I was hoping he would stay. I trust him, and I'm not sure I like the idea of us being separated while we sleep, anyway. Anything could happen. "I could sleep in the chair," I offer. "If you want the bed."

He frowns in confusion. "You wish me to stay?"

"I just… don't think it's a good idea to be separated while

the A'kai are still out there." It's not the entire truth, but it's not a lie either.

His brow furrows deeply, as if considering. "You… trust me this much?"

"Yes," I answer without hesitation. "I do."

His golden eyes search mine, something akin to hope reflecting behind them. "I will stay. But I will take the chair and you can have the bed."

I know I should argue, but I'm too exhausted. "All right."

A faint smile crests my lips as he places another fur over me to make sure I'm warm. "Thank you, Al'iro," I tell him, as I curl onto my side in the bed.

From what I could see on the computer, when he checked the weather, snow falls heavily around us, blanketing the entire area in a thick layer of white. I'm so glad we're safe and warm in here, but I'm worried about what happens when we leave.

The A'kai are still out there, and if we can't get ahold of Al'iro's people, we're going to have to walk back to his territory and risk being caught. I know he will do anything to protect me, but I don't want him to get hurt either.

I think of Elain and unbidden tears sting my eyes and blur my vision. I can't bear the thought of anyone else getting hurt for me.

I'm falling in love with him. I haven't known him very long, but it doesn't matter. This connection between us… it feels right in a way that nothing else ever has. And maybe it's crazy to feel this way, but what does it matter?

My mom always told me to follow my heart. I never listened before. I always allowed my mind to lead things. But, as I think of Al'iro, I cannot deny what I feel. It's too strong. Like some sort of cord wrapped tight around my heart and tethered to his.

Maybe this is what people mean when they speak of soul

mates. Maybe that's why I've never found love before. Maybe this is what I was supposed to find instead.

As I close my eyes, I send a silent prayer to whoever may be listening, to please give us a safe journey. I can't bear the thought of anything bad happening to him. Not now. Not after I've finally found someone to give my heart to.

CHAPTER 13

VIOLET

I close my eyes and fall straight into a nightmare.

Elain lies on the ground, bleeding. She lifts a pain-filled gaze to mine. "Go, Violet. Leave me."

"No." My voice quavers, tears streaming down my cheek. "I won't leave you."

"You have to!"

"I won't. Not again."

A menacing growl rumbles nearby. I turn and find glowing, green eyes full of malice staring down at me. The A'kai's lips pull back in a feral snarl, his eyes turning black, and he bares his fangs. "You cannot escape us. We are legion."

"No!" My eyes snap open, and I jerk up in bed.

My heart hammers against my ribcage as I scan the room, half expecting the A'kai to still be here.

Al'iro rushes into the room and moves to my side. "What's wrong?"

"I was having a nightmare... about the A'kai. And... Elain." My voice quavers.

He sits down beside me and takes my hand. "You are safe, Violet."

"I know," I whisper. "But deep down, I—"

"What is it?" he gently presses.

I lift my gaze to his. "I worry that the nightmares will never go away."

With a slight clench of his jaw, he lowers his gaze. "They may not."

I frown, surprised by his answer.

"They are wounds... scars that have been left on your heart. In time, they will lessen, but you will carry them always."

Tears fill his eyes. "My sister took her life because the nightmares were more than she could bear. Promise me that if you ever reach that point, you will come to me first."

"I promise," I whisper softly.

He lowers his gaze to his hands. "I should have seen the signs, but I did not."

"Al'iro, it wasn't your fault. Sometimes, people hide things... even from the ones they love. And they do it so well, that it's impossible to see."

As we sit together, I realize something. Both of us carry the guilt of the passing of another. Him for his sister and me for Elain.

Maybe that's another reason I feel so comfortable with him. We understand each other in a way that only someone who has experienced this sort of pain can understand another.

We sit in silence a moment longer before I lift my gaze to his. "When I woke up, you were gone. Where were you?"

"I was searching the other rooms for more clothing and supplies... some smaller boots that might fit you better." He sits in the chair next to the bed. "We are safe here. You do not have to worry. Even if they find the ship, they cannot get in."

"You're sure?"

"Yes."

Despite his reassurance, the images of my nightmare replay in my mind. Al'iro moves to stand, but I reach for him.

He stops abruptly, and turns back to me, a questioning look on his face.

My cheeks flare with heat as his golden eyes stare down at me intently. "Stay with me," I whisper. "Please."

His gaze darts to the bed, his brows drawing together in confusion, so I quickly add, "I mean... just to talk. Nothing else." *Not yet, anyway. And maybe not ever.*

"Of course."

Before I can say anything else, he pulls a chair up next to the bed. I love how he doesn't question me or make me feel embarrassed about asking him to do this. He simply... does it, just because I asked it of him.

"Are you hungry?" he asks.

I lift my hand and hold my forefinger close to my thumb. "A little."

"Ah." He holds up his hands and mimics the gesture. "Would you like a little bit of food or a lot?" When he says the words 'a lot,' he holds his two palms up as far apart as the width of his shoulders. He tips up his chin as a proud grin lights his face. "I have been observing Harry and studying the non-verbal communication of your species." He looks at his hands, still held apart. "Is this correct?"

I laugh softly. "Yes, it is, but... not everyone talks with their hands."

He frowns. "This is not... universal among your kind?"

A smile curls my lips. "No."

His grin falters, and his hands drop to his sides. "Oh."

"Some people are known for talking with their hands, and some do not do it at all." I pause, considering. "And some people only do it when they're trying to make a dramatic point or telling a story."

His brow furrows, his eyes dropping to the floor in a contemplative look. "So… not every Terran communicates in this way?"

"That's right."

"What about grasping hands and shaking them? Harry and Alana explained this is a common form of greeting among your people. Is this similar to how you take someone's measure?"

I blink. "Taking… someone's measure?"

"Yes. My people are able to take someone's measure when we take their hand, touching our palm to theirs. It is how we judge if their intentions are good or bad."

"You can tell that by touching someone's hand?"

He nods. "It is how I know the Mosaurans are not enemies, like we'd believed them to be not long ago."

"Why did you used to think they were bad?"

We both move to the couch, and we sit as he hands me a nutrient bar before he answers.

"There is a long history of bloodshed between our two species. They are a warrior race. Volatile… aggressive… but overall, they are honorable. I realize that now. We have formed an alliance with them; they are helping us to find your people."

He moves his chair close to the display console and taps the screen. Immediately, an image of a heavily muscled man with dark-gray wings and silver scales instead of skin appears. My mouth drifts open. "What is he?"

"A Mosauran," Al'iro explains.

With another tap of the screen, I watch as the man transforms from a two-legged form into something that looks like a huge and terrifying dragon. "A dragon," I whisper, more to myself than to him.

"This is their draken form."

He taps the screen again and another man appears. With tan skin, pointed, elf-like ears, and glowing, green eyes, he looks so similar to an A'kai, my jaw drops.

"That is a V'loryn. It is believed they share a common ancestor with the A'kai. But, they are very different species, however. The V'loryns are not savage like the A'kai."

"Good to know," I murmur.

He continues to scroll through other images of various species, explaining them to me. Some I recognize, like the Zovian and Anguis slavers, but others, I've never seen.

When the screen turns again to the Lycaon, I study it a moment. "It's strange."

"What is strange?"

"Their people look like werewolves, the Mosaurans like dragons, the V'loryns and A'kai like Vampires and Elves, and you,"—I turn my attention to him—"like the Fae. All of them are considered to be nothing more than products of imagination—the stuff of myths and legends on my world."

"Yes, Alana and Harry have said the same thing. I suspect our various species must have visited your world at some time in our history. It is the only explanation that makes sense."

"My mother used to tell me stories about the Fae when I was a child." A wistful smile curves my lips at the memory. "I remember it well."

"What kind of stories?" he asks, his expression curious.

"In the myths, the Fae are very handsome." A wistful smile curves my lips as I remember reading these stories when I was younger. "They would enchant and lure women into the woods, never to be seen again."

His expression falls. "Your people see us as monsters, then."

"Not always," I correct. "Most of the stories are romantic.

A handsome Fae prince falling in love with a Terran woman and taking her as his bride is usually how they turn out."

My cheeks heat as his golden eyes study me. "You enjoyed such stories?"

Slightly embarrassed, I lower my gaze. "Yes. I used to dream that a handsome Fae Prince would find me in the woods and offer to take me back to his castle."

He flashes a handsome grin. "I do not have a castle back on Aerilon, but my Estate is rather large." He takes my hand. "If we ever find a way off this ice world, I will take you there if you like."

"I would like that." I smile. "Tell me about your homeworld."

He sits back in his chair. "Aerilon is known as the jewel of the quadrant. At night, the plants and flowers glow with vibrant and beautiful bioluminescence in a varying array of colors. *Jaru* trees line the pathways along the gardens behind my home. Their trailing, purple vines sway gently in the breeze like living curtains around their trunks. Their flowers glow softly each night when the sun begins its slow descent into the horizon." He pauses. "It is believed these trees are blessed by the Fated Lovers."

"Fated Lovers?"

"Tr'omen and Kr'lena were the first rulers of our Empire. There is a Temple built for them because we believe they watch over and guide our people even now. It is beautiful," he says and it's easy to read the sadness in his expression. He's been stranded here for five years. It must be difficult to be gone for so long from his home.

"Many travel to the Temple, praying to the Fated Lovers that they may be blessed with a Fated One as well."

"What about you?" I ask. "Did you do this?"

A slight grin curls his lips. "You are here, are you not?"

I laugh softly, and he does too.

After a moment, his expression turns thoughtful. "It is strange to me that your people do not have fated bonds."

"Some people believe in soul mates," I explain. "They meet someone and just have a feeling… they know that person is supposed to be theirs."

"And you? Do you believe this?"

I don't tell him that before I was taken, I was a hopeless romantic who always prayed this would happen to me. I also do not tell him that, as he studies me with his golden eyes, something inside me tells me that that's what he is to me.

But part of me is afraid to voice this aloud. I'm not sure I'm ready to be completely intimate with someone, and I'm worried that if I tell him how I feel, he'll expect… something more. I know he said he would never pressure me, but… I'm still cautious.

We're so close, the warmth of his body radiates to mine. My gaze drops to his full, perfect lips, and I wonder what it would be like to kiss him again.

CHAPTER 14

AL'IRO

"And you?" I ask. "Do you believe this?"

"Yes," she says softly. "I do."

Her eyes search mine a moment, their color appearing green now. "Your eyes…. how is it they change color? Is this a phenotypic variation among your species?"

A soft puff of air escapes her in a laugh. "My eyes are hazel—a combination of green and light brown," she explains. "They sometimes appear green and sometimes brown, depending upon the light. It's their natural coloring."

I lean in a bit. "May I?"

She nods.

I move a bit closer, studying her eyes. The inner circle of the iris appears light-brown while the outer edge is flecked with a lovely green coloring. "They are stunning," I breathe. "A beautiful combination I have never encountered before."

A gorgeous smile curves her lips. "Your eyes are the ones that are stunning. I've never seen anyone with golden eyes before you."

I frown. "It is nothing special among my people. Our eyes are either gold or silver."

"Still," she says. "They're lovely." She smiles. "And your skin... the violet color is—"

"That is the name of the color you assign this shade?" I ask, pointing to my skin. "My people simply refer to it as purple."

She nods.

"How is it you were named after a color?"

"Violets are also flowers on my world. They were my mother's favorites. My father gave them to her on their first date."

"Date? Do you mean courtship?"

"Yes."

"My people also gift flowers in courtship. Many risk their lives to retrieve the rare purple blooms from the peaks of the *In'shara* mountains. They then present them to the one they desire to become their mate."

"Those flowers must be beautiful to be worth all the risk."

"Yes. They are rare and bloom only at night. It is breathtaking to view their glowing-purple light from afar."

"They glow as well?"

"Most of the plants on Aerilon are bioluminescent. Even the waters, when disturbed, glow with a brilliant blue light."

"Your world sounds so beautiful."

"It is. Most of the terrain on our world is mountainous, like it is here, but ours is covered in dense forests with vibrant flowers that glow in various shades of blues, purples, pinks, and yellows. The climate is temperate, and it rarely snows." I pause as a wistful smile crests my lips. "But, my favorite time of year is during the Harvest Festival."

"What is it like?" she asks, curiosity shining in her eyes.

"It is lovely. The city streets are decorated with festive banners and lined with stands of fresh fruits and vegetables and various crafts and wares. There is dancing and music and all manner of games." I sigh, nostalgia washing over me. "Ever since I joined the Aerilon Defense Force, I always make sure to put in for leave during that time because I do not wish to miss it."

She smiles. "It sounds amazing."

"Yes. People from all over the quadrant come to Aerilon for this festival."

"You mean… other species?"

"Yes. All races are accepted on my world. My people are one of the few that do not frown upon mixed species pairings."

A grin curves her lips. "Then, I will take you up on your offer to go to Aerilon. If we find a way off this planet, I'd love to see your world."

"I will take you then, someday."

She smiles. "I'd love that."

CHAPTER 15

AL'IRO

Violet sits beside me on the sofa and I cannot stop staring at the perfection of her full, pink lips, remembering the taste of her mouth when we kissed. I can already imagine a future with her by my side.

Without warning, the proximity alarm chimes, raising the hair on the back of my neck.

"What is that?" she asks, alarm in her voice.

My heart stops when I tap the console and it displays an A'kai right outside the ship.

She inhales sharply.

As the A'kai draws closer, he bares his fangs. His nostrils flare as he scents the air, no doubt searching for our location. He approaches the door, and I pray to the Creator he does not continue his advance, else he will run into the cloaked metal structure.

It would be difficult for him to get in, but not impossible.

Like the V'loryns, A'kai are possessed of excellent hearing. He should not be able to hear inside here, but I whisper anyway. "We must remain quiet."

"Does he know we're here?" she whispers.

"I do not know." I hate the fear in her eyes at my response. I wish I could reassure her, but I cannot. I do not know what led him here, but I suspect it was our scent. His people are excellent hunters. Their senses of smell, sight, and hearing are superior to almost every other species except the V'lo-ryns. They seem to be evenly matched in all ways.

A stifled growl builds in the back of my throat as my gaze remains locked on him. Fierce protectiveness moves through me, and I instinctively wrap my arm and wing around Violet, pulling her close to my side.

She is mine to protect, and I will not let anything happen to her.

CHAPTER 16

VIOLET

As the A'kai moves past the ship, I scoot closer to Al'iro. He wraps an arm around my waist and tugs me closer to him, wrapping his wing around my shoulder and side. I don't protest because it makes me feel safe and protected.

His wings may appear fragile like a dragonfly's, but they have the consistency of leather. When he tightens his wing even more, I nestle further into him as my heart hammers in my chest.

"He will not touch you, Violet," he states firmly. "Not while I draw breath."

His words ease away some of my fear, but they don't take it away entirely. I'm not just concerned for myself, I'm worried for him as well. The A'kai are dangerous and deadly.

After a few tense moments, the A'kai moves on. I watch in horror as he extends his nails into sharp claws and scales farther up the mountain. The moonlight reflecting off his monstrous form sends a chill down my spine.

"We are safe here," Al'iro whispers. "He has moved on."

Despite the fact the A'kai has left, fear coils tight in my chest, and I cannot sleep. I make no move to pull away from Al'iro, either. His solid, warm presence against me is comforting, and I am reluctant to leave the shelter of his wing around me.

Tenderly, he brushes the hair back from my face. "You should rest, Violet. I will keep watch."

I'm tired, but I doubt I'll be able to sleep now that I know the A'kai came so close.

"Why was he here? Do you think he followed our scent?"

Al'iro stills. "The tracking device," he whispers under his breath.

Panic fills me.

He turns his golden gaze to me. "I must scan you."

Gently, he lifts my hair and pulls it around the front, over my shoulder, as he runs a scanner over my back and neck. The signal it is emitting is a bit stronger than before for some reason."

He doesn't elaborate, but I assume it is probably because the A'kai is nearby, probably actively searching for the signal.

"In the morning, we can try using the MRU again. If the power cells have enough charge, I can remove it."

It's hard to fall asleep after seeing the A'kai so close to the ship. As far as I'm concerned, morning cannot come soon enough.

After a while, my eyes begin to blink closed as I struggle to stay awake.

"Sleep, Violet," Al'iro whispers. "I have you."

His tender words melt my heart because I know they're true. I curl up in his arms on the sofa and rest my head on his chest as I allow myself to drift away.

CHAPTER 17

VIOLET

I t is not yet dawn when I awaken. Al'iro moves to the console. He presses a series of commands, but it's no use.

"I cannot get a signal," he says defeatedly. "We cannot remain here any longer." He turns to me with a grim expression. "The A'kai found the door panel last night while you slept. He tried to pry off the panel to gain entrance, but I disabled it."

Terror fills me.

He continues. "We must try to remove your tracker before we leave."

Dark memories fill my mind as he powers up the MRU. I lie down in the bed, waiting for it to close over me when the entire thing shuts down with a low-pitched whine.

Frustrated, Al'iro clenches his jaw as he studies the

display. "The power cells are already drained. It seems they have deteriorated greatly since the last time I was here. I'll have to wait to remove your tracker when we get back to my people."

I was a ship's engineer. I'm used to dealing with tech problems. "Is there a way to block the signal if we can't remove the tracker?"

He frowns. "There might be. There is an ore on this world that disrupts our communicators. Aside from the storms, it is the main reason we have difficulty maintaining our communication signals." He turns to the computer console and taps the screen.

A map appears on the display. With a flick of his wrist, he projects the image toward me and points at a location. "We are here." He drags his finger across the terrain to a far point in the upper right corner. "This is where we must go—where my people are located."

"That seems pretty far."

"It is," he replies grimly. "But here"—he points to an area in between—"is a location we've found has heavy deposits of the ore that wreaks havoc on our signals." He pauses. "Normally, we avoid this area so we can continue to use our wrist comms. But, since I have lost mine, it does not matter. We can travel over this area to return to my people. It should mask your signal as well."

"Then, let's do that," I reply, hopeful.

"There is one problem."

"What?"

"Because it is a path I have not traveled before, it may be difficult to find shelter along the way. Your people are unable to regulate their body temperatures as effectively as mine. If we do not find shelter before the sun goes down each day, we would risk—"

"Me freezing to death," I finish his sentence.

With a slight clench of his jaw, he nods.

I glance around the room. "Any chance this ship folds up like a tent so we can take it with us?" I ask, half-teasing, but praying it does by some miraculous innovation of technology.

He shakes his head. He turns and gestures to the screen. An image of the valley below this cliff appears. He points to a path between two large mountains in the distance. "That is where we must go."

My lips part on an inhale because it seems like it's really far away.

"Beyond that pass is our territory. If anything happens to me, that is where you must go. Do you understand?"

"Yes."

Silence settles in the space between us, and my thoughts turn again to the A'kai. "Do you think he'll follow us?"

"Yes." He pauses. "You should rest before the sun rises. We might have some advantage if we leave at first light. The more daylight we have for travel, the better. The A'kai possess superior night vision."

I swallow against the knot of worry in the pit of my stomach and settle down in the bed, turning onto my side facing Al'iro and curling up beneath the furs. This is likely to be the last bit of good sleep I'll have over the next several days, so I'd better enjoy it while I can.

An image of the A'kai outside the ship fills my mind, and I shudder inwardly. Sensing my distress, Al'iro turns to me. "I will use my wings to glide down from the mountain. That should at least give us a head start."

"But, won't that hurt you?" I ask, concerned.

"It is worth the pain."

Guilt overcomes me, and I reach for his hand, gently taking it in mine. He leans forward and presses a tender kiss to my forehead. "I will pack our things while you rest."

CHAPTER 18

VIOLET

When I wake, I find Al'iro already moving about the room. He has two large packs open on the floor, and I watch as he stuffs them full of supplies—one more so than the other. It's still dark outside, and I wonder how long it is until dawn.

I sit up in the bed, and his head snaps to me. "We still have another hour until daylight if you'd like to sleep longer."

I shake my head. "I don't think I can. I'm too nervous."

His expression softens, and he nods. "Here." He hands me a plate with what appears to be strips of dried meat. "You should eat before we leave."

I would ask what it is but realize it doesn't matter. I cannot afford to be picky. Food is fuel. That has been my motto ever since I was taken. I have to eat to keep up my strength. I thank him, and start to eat.

It reminds me of jerky but without any sort of flavoring. To be honest, it's better than what we were served as slaves. "I found more nutrient bars," he says, gesturing to one of the packs. "Your people require more than just meat, I have learned. So, we are currently working on creating a 'greenhouse'—I believe Alana called it—"to grow edible plants for your people."

"I studied botany before I became an engineer," I tell him, glad to find another use for my skillset. "So, I could help with it."

"Vorek will be very glad for his mate to have help with this. He feels that Alana takes on too much as it is."

"Vorek—the guy Alana is with… is he… nice?"

A smile curls Al'iro's lips. "Very much so. He is an excellent mate to her. I have even caught him smiling every now and then."

I frown. "And that's unusual for him to smile?"

"Yes. His people—the V'loryns—are the ones who rarely show any outward emotion. They are taught to suppress it from the time they are young."

I can't imagine what that must be like: to have a husband who doesn't express emotion, but I also know Alana. She wouldn't settle down with someone unless she were truly in love. "I'm glad she found someone."

Al'iro's eyes meet mine and I realize how easily he could be *my* someone too. If only I'd let him.

"Should we try the MRU again?" I ask.

His expression turns grim. "I already checked. The power cells are not charged enough. It seems their capacity is far less than it was the last time I came to this ship."

Devastation along with a heavy dose of fear floods my system, but I force myself to push it back down. We can make it. We have to.

"When should we leave?"

He taps on the console to view the outside of the ship, providing a glimpse of the valley below us.

A soft, orange glow is just barely visible as dawn approaches. "Soon. But first, I must give you this."

He holds out something that looks like one of the blasters I stole from the A'kai and lost in the river. It's slightly different, but appears similar enough.

"You are familiar with this."

I recognize the question in his statement. "Yes. And I'm a pretty decent aim, if that's what you're asking."

His lips quirk up slightly. "It is." He gestures to the blaster. "Here are the settings." He shows me the various symbols. "This one is for stun and this one for kill."

His gaze meets mine evenly. "Keep it easily accessible at all times. And do not hesitate to use it."

"I won't."

"Come. I must outfit you with more layers to keep you warm."

He directs me to stand with my arms out to my side as he uses his claws to cut holes in the furs from the bedding and then wraps them around me. He layers four of these over me, and that's on top of two makeshift pants he hastily crafted from what he found in crew quarters.

By the time he's finished, I look like I'm three times my size.

"How is that?" he asks.

I waddle across the room. "I feel like a puffball, but at least I'm warm."

He frowns. "A… 'puffball.' I have heard this term before from Alana. Is it a type of animal on Terra?"

I laugh. "No… it's more of an expression. It means I feel like I'm huge."

"Ah," he says, understanding registering on his face. "I believe I can trim some of this material under your arms. Perhaps, that will help."

I hold out my arms as he trims it away and then loops a belt around it all so it's now an impromptu, over-large tunic. I swing my arms, glad I have more movement. "This is great. Thanks."

He nods, then sits back, considering. "Now, we must cover your feet."

He pulls out a set of boots and gives me an apologetic look. "These are the smallest I could find."

He observes as I put them on. "Your feet are so small," he murmurs. "Is this... normal for your kind? I thought Alana and Harry might be an exception."

I laugh. "They are normal size, thank you very much."

With the fur he placed to line the inside, It's not easy to walk in my boots, but again... it's warm, so I'm not going to complain.

His brow furrows when he studies me.

"What's wrong?"

"We have far to travel, and your outfit and footwear are not conducive to much walking."

I tip up my chin. "I've been through survival training in the Terran space program. They taught us to make do with what we have. I'll be fine. I promise. I won't slow you down."

His gaze holds mine as he gives me a warm smile. "You are not a burden, my Al'essa. Never, for a moment, believe that you are."

A warm flush creeps up my neck to my face at his tender words and his gaze. I cup his cheek and lean in to brush my lips to his in a gentle kiss.

He drops his forehead to mine and then pulls me close, wrapping his arms and wings around me. "All will be well, my Al'essa. I will keep you safe."

CHAPTER 19

VIOLET

I watch as Al'iro makes a cloak for himself out of two furs and slips the heaviest pack over his shoulders. Turning to peer outside, I notice the early morning rays of the sun filtering into the forest below us.

If I wasn't so afraid, I'd probably think this view is stunning, with the thick forest of pine-like trees with red-orange needles and the entire valley blanketed in snow.

I take Al'iro's hand as we stand in front of the viewscreen, looking out the ship. It's warm in here, but I know the moment we step outside, it's going to probably be freezing again.

Gently, he squeezes my hand. "Are you ready, my Al'essa?"

I like that he calls me this and I give him a warm smile. "Yes."

I reach for one of the packs, huffing a bit as I haul it onto my back. He eyes me a moment, and I just know he's going to probably insist he can carry it, but I don't want to add to his burden. He's already going to be hurting after he uses his injured wings to glide off the mountain. So, I quickly say, "I'm good, Al'iro. I've got this."

His eyes travel over me once more, and it is easy to read the concern on his face as he pulls the fur hood over my head and gently tucks my hair inside.

Just that extra bit of care, he takes with me, melts my heart. I'm falling in love with this man. How is it that I can already feel this way for someone I only just met?

I could question it. I could tell myself I'm crazy. But instead, I decide to embrace it. I used to believe in fate… and maybe it's time I believed in something again. So, I stretch up on my toes and press a tender kiss to his lips.

He flashes a devastatingly handsome smile. "What was that for?"

"Just because," I murmur.

He gives me a teasing grin. "That is an excellent reason."

Together, we stand in front of the door. He lifts his palm to place it on the control pad but pauses and turns to me. "If anything should happen, I want you to leave me behind. Keep going toward the mountain pass, like I showed you on the screen."

"No. I won't."

He blinks in surprise.

Tears sting my eyes at the memory of Elain. "Don't ask me to do this, because I won't. Elain asked me to leave her behind, and it was the hardest thing I've ever had to do." I swallow against the lump in my throat. "I'll never leave anyone behind again."

I draw in a deep breath. "I was afraid and I ran for my life when she told me to go. But I won't do this again. I won't, Al'iro. If I could take back that moment I would. So… don't ask this of me."

"I do not want you to risk yourself for me, Violet. Please do not—"

"No," I move to his side and take his hand. "Whatever fate awaits us, we will meet it together. I will never leave anyone behind ever again."

His gaze holds mine, and he gives me a reluctant nod. He cups my chin and then gently drops his forehead to my own. "Whatever fate awaits us, we will meet it together," he repeats my words like a solemn vow.

He gathers me close to his chest for a moment before stepping back. He places his palm on the panel, and the door slides open. "Let us go."

CHAPTER 20

AL'IRO

The moment the door slides open, a blast of cold air hits us full force. Violet shivers against it, and I grit my teeth. Terrans are much more fragile than my people, and I worry for her. The wind claws at us when we step outside, the snow falling heavily all around us.

We walk around the ship toward the cliff edge, and I study the valley below, trying to gauge the best approach to glide toward it, when a sinister growl rumbles behind us.

I spin, and my heart stops when I see the A'kai, baring his fangs as his nails lengthen into deadly claws. "I knew you could not hide forever, Aerilon," he snarls. "Give me the Terran. Now."

The acrid scent of Violet's fear floods my nostrils, calling forth my protective instincts. I grip her forearm and pull her behind me. "Never."

Lightning fast, he races toward us.

I only have a moment to spin around. Gathering her in

my arms, I leap from the cliff wall, and we tumble over the side.

Violet's scream echoes through the forest as we fall toward the ground with dizzying speed.

It takes every ounce of my strength to extend my wings. Pain arcs through my back like fire as they snap open and catch the wind. I hold her tightly to my chest, gritting my teeth as I ride the current, trying to direct our path as far away from the mountain as I can.

The anger-filled roar of the A'kai, raging at our escape, follows after us.

We have a head start on him, but I know it is not much. His people are capable of speeds greater than mine. I worry he'll be upon us sooner than I expect.

Violet's eyes are wide as she stares at the snow-covered forest below. A gust of wind lifts us higher a moment, granting us further distance.

As it wanes, I do my best to control our landing, not wanting to injure her. Carefully, I set down upon one of the upper tree branches. This one is as wide as two people, and I know it will hold my weight as we survey the area below.

The A'kai are not the only beings that hunt on this planet. I must be mindful of other predators. Snowcats are plentiful in these woods and capable of moving with great stealth. I doubt Violet would survive an attack from one of these vicious creatures—their claws are lethal and sharp as daggers. I have seen them rend flesh from bone as they take down one of their kills.

I shudder inwardly at the thought of one of them hurting Violet.

I turn my sharp gaze to the forest, listening for any sounds of predators or enemies, but hear none.

She looks over the edge of the branch, eyes widening slightly. "It's a long way down," she murmurs.

"I will carry you. Can you hold onto me?"

She nods.

I move closer and observe as her cheeks flush a deep, reddish hue as she wraps her arms and legs around me, facing me. My protective instincts flare as she clings tightly to me. Her smaller form calls to something deep and primal within me—a desire to protect and defend her against any and all danger. She is mine. My Al'essa. And I promise to protect her.

With her chest pressed against mine, I can feel the rapid fluttering of her heart. Gently, I nuzzle her hair.

She lifts her eyes to mine. They are green in this light, I notice.

My nostrils flare as I take in her delicate scent. Something akin to the ilani flowers back on my home world.

"Do you think he can track me here?" she asks.

"He should not be able to. This is the area I showed you on the map. It is lined with the ore that disrupts communication signals. It should dampen the tracker's signal should he try to access it."

Her shoulders visibly relax at my words, and I'm grateful to offer her at least some measure of comfort.

When we reach the ground, I carefully lower her feet to the snow. She loses her balance, and I grip her hand to steady her.

As I do, heat travels across my palm as I inadvertently take her measure. I detect an underlying current of fear. But beneath that, I recognize something different. An emotion akin to caring but not quite. It feels like something more...

I still as I realize what it is.

Love.

Her desire and longing match that of my own.

My eyes dart to hers, and she quickly averts her gaze as pink blooms across the bridge of her nose and cheeks.

I glance back at my wings, surprised they have not started glowing, even despite my injury. The pull I feel to her is so strong, it is nearly overwhelming. Then again, I suppose it is a small blessing that they do not glow. It would be difficult to hide with my wings lit up like a beacon for every creature in the forest to notice.

A small noise ahead makes me still. I gather Violet close and listen close, trying to determine what it is.

CHAPTER 21

VIOLET

A l'iro goes still and then pulls me to his chest. I remain silent as he scans the forest all around us. Up ahead, I see something move.

He instantly relaxes. "It is a snow hare." He points to it, and sure enough it looks something like a cross between a rabbit and a squirrel with two long ears and a fluffy white tail. "They are harmless."

My heart clenches as it lifts its little head and sniffs the air with its cute nose. "It's so precious," I tell him.

"Yes," he grumbles. "Until they decide to make a nest in the ship's wiring."

I laugh.

"It took three days to relocate them."

"Relocate?" I ask, hoping this isn't some sort of code word for *exterminate*.

He nods. "We had to carry them all several arcums away so they would not make their way back to us."

I smile because it tells me the people I'll be living with have tender hearts toward innocent creatures.

As we make our way through the forest, I'm struck again by how similar the trees are to the great pine trees on Terra but with orange-red needles instead of green. Flakes of snow whirl and dance on the breeze. I would probably think it lovely if I weren't so cold.

It's only been a few hours, but I already miss the warmth and protection of the ship. Out here, I feel so exposed and on edge. Every little movement in the corner of my eye makes my heart pound with worry.

A frigid breeze blows through the woods, and the branches sway back and forth—their movement startling me —and I move closer to Al'iro's side.

He's taller than me. The top of my head barely level with his chin. I allow my gaze to travel over his broad shoulders and heavily muscled physique. He's so handsome. Like a marble statue of masculine perfection.

I glance back at his broken wings, the soft light catching the clear membranes, scattering colorful patterns on the ground beside us. I pray the Healers will be able to repair them.

I notice he keeps them tucked close to his back. They must pain him terribly. I hate I'm the reason they're broken.

"Alana says there are trees similar to these back on your world," he says.

"Yes, but not quite as tall and impressive as these," I add. "This place does remind me of the Alaskan wilderness, though."

He frowns.

"An area of Terra with a climate like this: snow, cold temperatures... I always dreamed of going there. I have heard it is beautiful, but I never got around to it."

"There is a place on Aerilon with trees similar to this. During the warmer months of the cycle, they develop beautiful blooms of light pinks and reds. They are high up in the In'shara mountains." A wistful smile crests his lips. "I have a home up there. A place that has been in my family for many generations. I would often go there when I was on Aerilon for my leave."

"What would you do up there?"

"It is the one place where I can be at peace. Where nothing is expected of me. Not duty or protocols or engagement with others." He pauses, trudging forward a few more steps. "Up there... I can simply be." His eyes brighten with tears. "My family and I used to spend a lot of time there, when my sister and I were children."

"It sounds lovely. My family had a cabin in the woods, too. We used to go every weekend during the summers. It was close to a lake, and we used to swim almost every day before my parents got divorced."

"Divorced?" He frowns. "This word is not translating for me. What does it mean?"

"Separated," I explain. "No longer married."

"I had forgotten that your people do not mate for life," he murmurs, more to himself than to me.

"Yours do?"

"Yes."

"That must be nice," I muse. "To know for sure the person you pick is going to stay with you forever. If Terrans were that way, I probably wouldn't have put off looking for someone to spend my life with."

"You were afraid you would find a mate, and they would leave you?"

I shrug. "I guess after seeing how my dad left my mom, it was always in the back of my mind that the same could someday happen to me, you know. And I didn't want to go through that. The heartache and the pain... It was really hard on my mother."

He turns to me. "Are your parents still alive?"

"My mom died a few years ago. But my dad... I don't know what happened to him. After he left, he never came back. Not even to see me."

Al'iro's eyes widen in shock. I'm guessing from his expression that this doesn't happen on Aerilon.

I'm glad. At least I know that if I decided to be with him, it wouldn't be a temporary thing. He wouldn't just get tired of being married and decide to leave.

"What about your parents?" I ask. "Are they... back on Aerilon?"

He sighs. "I worry for them. They lost my sister and then... me."

I thread my fingers through his. "I'm sorry."

"I have not yet given up hope of seeing them again," he says.

I like that he says this. It means he's someone who clings to hope instead of despair.

As we continue through the woods, we talk back and forth about our lives. It's so easy to talk to him that time seems to pass quickly. Before I know it, the sun is already low in the horizon.

He scans the forest. "We should search for shelter."

"Where?" I ask, hoping he has some idea where we might find somewhere to sleep that's not out in the open.

He lifts his gaze. "The trees."

"What?"

His wings flutter uselessly at his side, and he sighs heavily. "We will have to climb."

CHAPTER 22

VIOLET

I wrap my arms and legs around his front, and he begins to climb. I'm surprised by how quickly he scales the large tree and how easily he carries me—as though I weigh nothing. The trees on this world may be similar to pines, but some are so large, they remind me of the great sequoias.

As we near the top, he stops and surveys our surroundings. His eyes widen slightly at something in the distance, and he wraps his arms tightly around me. "Hold on."

Before I can ask any questions, he leaps from one tree to another, landing squarely on a large branch. My gaze drops to the forest floor below, heart hammering in my chest as I consider just how far down it would be if we fell.

His nostrils flare. "I can scent your fear, Violet." He nuzzles my temple. "I promise I will not drop you."

Unable to speak, I swallow against the knot of worry in my stomach and barely manage to nod.

He walks on the branch toward the massive trunk, and I

notice an opening—large enough for us to crawl inside. "We will shelter in there."

I blink at him. "What about the A'kai. Won't they find us if they're nearby? Their sense of smell is—"

"The trees secrete a sap in openings like these. It will mask our scent." He starts for the opening but stops and looks at me. "I suggest you are mindful of the interior walls. The sap is rather difficult to remove once it adheres to clothing and skin."

"Noted." I grin. I'm relieved the stuff even exists. If it can mask our scent from the A'kai, I'm seriously considering slathering it all over me. I'll definitely sleep better tonight.

He stops just at the entrance. "I'll go in first to make certain nothing else is inside."

Panic crawls up my spine. "Like what?"

"Razor birds," he says.

I don't like the sound of that...

"Why do you call them 'razor birds?' "

"Their beaks are—"

I lift my hands up. "Got it. I... don't think I want to know anymore. Not if I'm going to sleep tonight."

He cups my chin, tipping my face up to his as he gives me a solemn look. "Do not worry. I will not let one eat you."

My jaw drops, but I quickly snap it shut and arch a brow. "You *do* realize that sentence was not as reassuring as I think you intended for it to be, right?"

His brows pinch together. "You doubt my strength?"

"I-no, I just... hadn't even considered it might try to eat me until you brought it up."

"Ah," he says, understanding spreading across his features. "In truth, it would probably not try to eat you. It would probably only try to maim you, instead. Perhaps, take a limb or some such."

My mouth drifts open as he turns away and carefully

enters the opening in the trunk. That last sentence wasn't very reassuring either. Panic squeezes my chest as I wait for him to emerge again.

When he does, he smiles, and my heart stutters an erratic beat for an entirely different reason besides fear. "It is clear," he says. "You may enter now."

I crawl inside, surprised by how spacious it is. We may not be able to stand, but we can still comfortably sit, and there is enough space for us to sleep in the center, away from the sticky sap lining the walls.

I brush a finger over the sap, wondering about the feasibility of covering myself in it for the rest of our trek, and quickly decide against it. I'm fairly certain I'd never get it off.

There's enough light that I can see Al'iro clearly, so I'm surprised when he removes his fur cloak and the tunic beneath, leaving his upper body completely bare.

My eyes wander over the thick cords of muscle lining his abdomen and chest. He is every fantasy I ever had of the Fae. His golden eyes meet mine, and I realize I'm gaping as he offers me his clothes. "Wha-what about you? Won't you be cold?"

"It is sheltered enough in here that I should be all right for the night. Here," he carefully drapes the tunic and fur cloak over me, "you will need this to keep you warm."

He lies down beside me but with some distance between us.

Despite the layers of fur, I'm still so cold that I'm miserable. "We're not going to sleep together?" I ask, cursing inwardly when I realize I've said this aloud.

He blinks several times. "I thought you would prefer—"

"For warmth," I add quickly. "Terrans... we usually sleep together, I mean, next to each other, for warmth when it's cold."

"Holding each other?" he asks, studying me intently.

"Yes."

He moves closer, and I lift the fur cloak just enough to cover us both as I curl into him, all modesty and embarrassment forgotten as I snuggle against him for warmth.

I press my hands to his torso and my feet to his shins as I bury my face in his chest. He smells so good. I breathe deep of his masculine scent.

He wraps his arms around me, holding me close, and then his wings curl around us both. I marvel again at their leathery texture.

A soft sigh of contentment escapes me, because I feel so warm and safe in his arms and wings. "I have not told you something about the bond," he whispers into my hair.

"What is it?"

He pulls back just enough to meet my eyes. "Fated mates are often able to sense one another's emotions, especially if they are strong. This can happen even before they seal the bond."

"Oh," I tell him, not sure how to respond. "Does that mean you can read my mind?"

"No, but I sense something from you right now. But I am uncertain what it is." He tucks a stray tendril of hair behind my ear. "What were you thinking of just now?"

I hesitate, not sure how much to say. After a moment, I decide to simply tell the truth. "Being with you like this… it feels right in a way that nothing else ever has. As if by simply being here in your arms… I'm home."

He cups my cheek. "I feel the same."

CHAPTER 23

AL'IRO

I am in awe of her trust in me. She has been through so much, and yet, I feel honored she is comfortable enough to be this close to me. She snuggles against me and happiness blooms in my chest.

Something deep and primal rises within me as I hold her close, as if she were already mine. My mate. Mine to protect and hold and cherish.

Inhaling deeply, I draw her delicate scent into my lungs and commit it to memory. I have flown with her twice now. Although it was merely gliding, each time it called to something within me. A female Aerilon only allows a male to carry her if he is her mate.

She looks to me. "Does this get stronger after the bond is sealed?"

"I have heard that it does."

"How do you seal the bond?"

My entire body flushes with warmth. "The first mating seals it... usually the mating flight."

Her brows go up. "Mating flight?"

"Yes. The male will present his wings to the female and then drop to one knee before her, asking her to choose him. If she does, he gathers her in his arms and they take off into the air for their first mating."

"While flying?" her voice rises a bit in pitch.

I nod.

"A bonded pair… their first flight together is after she has chosen him as hers. Only then does a female trust a male to carry her."

Violet's gaze holds mine as she reaches out to touch my face. She traces her delicate fingers over my brow and to the sensitive tips of my ears. When she moves her hands down to the inner lining of my wings, a small shudder runs through me.

She jerks her hand away. "Did I hurt you?"

"An Aerilon's wings are very sensitive," my voice comes out a bit rougher than I'd expected. "They are erogenous zones."

"Oh," she says, her cheeks flushing red.

Through our connection, I note a small sliver of worry. Gently, I brush my lips against her in a tender kiss. "I will never touch you against your will."

"I know," she whispers, her eyes bright with tears.

I wrap my wings tighter around her and hold her close. "I will keep you safe, my Al'essa. Now rest, while I keep watch."

She nestles even closer to me, and a small trill of contentment thrums deep in my chest.

CHAPTER 24

AL'IRO

When I wake in the morning, Violet is still asleep in my arms and wings. I move slightly, and my heart clenches as she nestles even closer.

Gently, I tighten my wings around her and run a hand over her long hair, the strands soft beneath my fingers. I am struck again by how delicate her features are, and anger fills me at the thought of all she endured.

Despite the fragility of her form, she is strong in other ways, I realize. In my time on the Aerilon Defense Force, I have taken care of many former slaves. So many of them, like my sister, with the faraway stare that speaks of great suffering and trauma. I have seen this look on Violet's face, but I have also seen something else. She still smiles, despite all she has been through.

She still clings to hope. Hope is a rare thing when you are a slave. I realize, now, I had lost this—the ability to hope for anything for myself. I thought the Creator had cursed me by abandoning me on this world.

But as I hold Violet in my arms, I realize now that this is why I was here. It was so that our paths would cross as they were meant to.

As I study Violet, sleeping in my arms, it is as if that part of me has been reawakened. For the first time in many cycles, I have hope. Not just that we might someday escape this world... but hope for a future as well.

I sigh heavily when I remember that she has not chosen me as hers yet. Despite my attempts to temper this spark in my chest, I cannot. I desire more than anything to be her mate.

Gently, she stirs in my arms. Her eyelids flutter open, and she gives me a sleepy smile. Her warm, hazel eyes appear green in the soft morning light filtering into our nest as she gazes at me.

She stretches her lithe form against mine and my *lvost* lengthens and extends with want to join my body to hers. I shift and angle my hips away from her, not wanting to scare her with my body's reaction to her nearness.

"Are you hungry?" I ask.

She nods. As she sits up, I allow my arms and wings to fall away. I search our emergency packs and hand her two strips of dried meat. When I offer her the nutrient bar, she declines. "You should eat," I tell her. "You have not eaten much since we have been together."

"I don't think my stomach can handle too much food just yet. It's gotten so used to not having much that I don't want to risk getting sick."

Her reasoning is sound, even as rage twists deep inside me at the thought of how she was starved before. This has only strengthened my conviction that we must hunt down all the A'kai and end them.

For the past five cycles, we have kept to ourselves and left them alone in their territory. But now that more have crashed on this world, we cannot continue in this way. They are a danger to Violet and her people. The Terrans will only be safe after we have eliminated them all.

After a quick first meal, I carefully move outside of our shelter. She remains inside as I scan the forest and listen for any signs of the A'kai, or other predators, nearby.

My nostrils flare as I detect the scent of a snowcat, but it is faint. It must have passed through here during the night.

When I am satisfied it is safe, I turn to Violet and motion for her to come out. She holds on to me as we climb down from the tree to the ground.

Carefully, I place her on her feet. As I move to take her pack from her, she shakes her head. "I can carry it, Al'iro."

"It is no burden for me."

She steps closer and takes my hand. "You've already done so much. Please, I want to help. I don't want you to have to carry all this weight on your own."

"From what I have discovered of Terran anatomy, my people possess two to three times the strength of yours. It is not difficult, in the slightest, for me to carry both packs."

I reach for the pack again, and she reluctantly hands it over. As I take it from her, I notice how she straightens her spine. I am glad I can carry this for her. It is easy to see it would have been a great burden for her, in her current state. It will take time for her body to recover from all the abuse she endured during her enslavement.

My gaze darts to her neck and the two healing puncture wounds left there by the A'kai. I cannot wait to get her back to my people and behind our force shield wall. Only then, will I know she is truly safe.

As we walk through the woods, I remain alert for any signs

we are being followed. Even without the tracker's signal, the A'kai are excellent hunters.

"You said that everything on the V'loryn ship still works, except the engines, right?" she asks, pulling me back from my dark thoughts.

"That is correct."

"So... between the five different ships that crashed, there weren't enough pieces to get one of them running again?"

I frown, considering her question, uncertain how to answer. "We scavenged what we could from our ship, before we moved into the V'loryn vessel, but the others... we have been unable to determine what the state of their ships are. Aside from being unable to break atmosphere, that is."

"Unable to determine or... you just didn't ask?"

"In truth, we did not ask. It is only recently that we have an... agreement between us—the Aerilon and V'loryns—and now the Mosaurans. Before your people came along, the rest of us did our best to avoid each other."

"Why?"

"Our species are not exactly on good terms."

"And the A'kai? Do they hunt your people, as well?"

"Not on this world."

"But, they're blood drinkers. How do they survive?"

"It may seem like a cold and desolate world, but there are many animals that make their home here. I suspect that is how they... supplement their diets."

Something up ahead catches my eye, and I raise my arm out to stop Violet as I still.

"What is it?" she whispers, her expression full of fear.

"A snowcat. It is stalking us."

Three choices lie before me: I could stay here and hope that it leaves, but I doubt it will. I could fight it, but I do not know if it is alone—they often hunt in packs. Or I could run."

I dart a glance at Violet. "We're going to run," I whisper urgently.

Lightning fast, I gather her in my arms.

The snowcat lunges from behind a felled trunk and charges toward us as I break into a run.

The powdered snow is like shifting sand beneath my feet as I race through the forest. The crunch of ice and snow behind me from its pursuit grows louder, and my heart thunders in my chest when I notice two more rush in from either side.

The dull roar of rushing water up ahead gives me hope. Snowcats will not cross bodies of water. They hate it.

As I run toward it, I am not sure what we'll find, but I have no choices. If I were alone, I would probably stand and fight them, but I cannot risk Violet. I doubt I would be able to fight and defend her at the same time.

Violet shifts in my arms and glances over my shoulder. "I think I can hit them."

I open my mouth to ask what she means when she pulls the blaster from her belt and aims it over my shoulder. The click of the discharge is quickly followed by the sharp jerk of her body from the recoil as she fires a blast.

An angry roar fills the woods when it hits its mark.

"I got one," she cries out.

My pulse pounds in my ears as I hold tightly to Violet, the muted roar of the water growing louder as we race toward it. Up ahead, I notice a river and a large waterfall, but no way to safely cross.

It is too wide, and even if we tried to swim, I doubt we would make it across without going over the falls. The current looks strong and the water is too turbulent. We'll have no choice but to jump from the top of the waterfall and glide down to the area below.

Bracing myself for the inevitable pain of using my wings, I jump.

Sharp claws dig into my flesh and my wings and I cry out as Violet tumbles from my arms as I slam to the ground.

"No!" I roar as she rolls toward the edge.

I twist onto my back, shaking off the snowcat. We clash in a tangled mass of fangs and claws. I sink my teeth deep into its neck, injecting it with my venom.

The snowcat releases a painful cry, then goes limp, paralyzed by the bite, and I fling it over the falls, sending it to its death below.

Another rushes forward and I wrap my arms tight around its neck. It twists and writhes beneath me before I throw it aside.

It hits a nearby boulder with a sickening crunch and falls still.

Without warning, another snowcat barrels into my chest, forcing the air from my lungs and slamming me to the ground. It lunges at me again, but Violet moves in my path and fires at it with her blaster.

It hits the snowcat's shoulder, knocking it back.

She moves to aim again, but it attacks, swiping its massive paw across her torso, claws tearing through her fur coverings like paper. The blaster flies from her hand, clattering against stone before sliding over the side of the cliff wall.

Rage floods my system as the bittersweet scent of her blood hits the air so strong it overpowers my nostrils. I rush toward the snowcat, throwing it to the ground.

It struggles and somehow manages to twist beneath me, forcing me onto my back, snarling and snapping its razor-sharp teeth at my face.

My arms shake from exertion at the struggle to hold it back.

Out of the corner of my eye, I watch as Violet slams into its side, forcing it away from me.

It spins and catches her with its massive paws, and I watch in horror as they start to fall off the side of the cliff. Her hazel eyes meet mine, full of fear, a moment before she disappears, tumbling over the edge.

"No!" I cry out, pushing myself off the edge and diving for her, arms outstretched.

Her eyes hold mine as we continue to fall. I watch as she slams into the water, and it envelopes her, swallowing her whole.

A moment later, I crash through the surface, spinning and tumbling away in the swift current. I grasp her arm firmly and pull her to me, kicking my legs furiously, fighting to swim to the surface.

As soon as we break through, she gasps, desperate for air. I haul us both to the shore. Her body shivers uncontrollably from the cold, and I scan our surroundings. I have to find shelter, and I need to get her warm. Now.

I notice a yawning cave mouth on one side of the falls, near the pool at the bottom. Gathering Violet in my arms, I rush toward it. As soon as we enter, I'm greeted by a warm steam rising from the floor.

Our study of this planet has revealed several warm springs scattered throughout the various territories we have charted. It seems this cave is connected to one because it is warm. I rush to the back of the cave with Violet in my arms, and drop to my knees.

"You're going to be all right, my Al'essa."

She gives me a weak nod as she shivers.

Quickly, I peel away all of Violet's clothing, glad when I notice the claws of the snowcat did not reach her skin through the heavy layers of fur she had on. I open one of the emergency packs, thankful we did not lose them in the water, and pull out an emergency blanket.

She shivers uncontrollably as I wrap it around her smaller form. "This should warm you."

She barely manages to nod, unable to speak around her chattering teeth.

I search through the other bag, breathing a sigh of relief when I find the other emergency blanket. I quickly throw off my clothes and gather her in my arms, pulling her into my lap and leaning against the wall, where the surrounding stone feels the warmest, as I wrap my arms and wings, and the blankets, around us both.

CHAPTER 25

VIOLET

Shivering in Al'iro's lap, completely naked, I press my hands to his torso and bury my face against his chest. He's so warm, he's like a personal furnace. Normally, I'd probably feel embarrassed to be undressed like this, but not now. Right now, I'm too cold. Besides, I trust him. He would never take advantage of me.

After my body stops shaking, I lift my head to his. "Are you all right?"

"Yes." I lift my arm to hers to show her the claw marks are already beginning to heal. My kind heal much more quickly than hers. "Are you warm now?"

I nod in return, frowning when his expression turns thunderous. "Do not ever do that again," he says in a low voice, laced with quiet anger.

I jerk back. "Do what?"

"Risk yourself for me like that," he snaps. "You could have been killed."

"So could you," I snap back. "What was I supposed to do? Watch you die?"

"You should have run—tried to save yourself, like I told you before we left."

I shake my head. "And I already told you I was *never* leaving anyone behind again. That includes you." I press my finger to his chest for emphasis. "So, I don't care if you're mad. I wasn't going to leave you to die. Not like Elain. Never again."

His expression softens. "Forgive me. I should not have gotten angry at you. I just—" he hesitates a moment before continuing, "I understand you lost someone. I did, too," he says, and I realize he is speaking of his sister. "I feel the same way as you. I would rather give my life than ever lose someone again. But I love you, Violet. I cannot bear the thought of losing you."

He draws in a shaking breath. "When I watched you go over the edge—" his voice catches. "I cannot lose you, my Al'essa. I love you too much."

I glance at his wings wrapped around us, noting the areas that still appear broken. I cannot imagine how much it must still pain him. "You've already sacrificed so much for me, Al'iro. It's my fault you might never fly again. I—"

"I would change nothing that has happened between us," he says. "Even if I never regain the use of my wings, I will never regret saving you, Violet. I used to believe the Creator had forsaken me when we crashed on this planet. But now I understand. He put me here so that I could find you, my Al'essa. And all this time I thought I was cursed, when, in truth, I am the most blessed of all males."

Gently, he leans in and presses a series of tender kisses to my cheeks, nose and brow. "You are mine to protect and cherish. And even if you never choose me in return, I ask only to remain at your side."

He cups my chin and his golden eyes meet mine evenly. "I want only to be whatever you need. Even if it means you never choose me as yours."

My heart clenches at his words and the tender way he holds me. I take his hand in mine. "You said you could feel in your heart that we are fated. Well, I can feel it too. This," I place his hand to my heart, "feels right, my love. In a way that nothing ever has before. A tear escapes my lashes and he brushes it away with the soft pad of his thumb. "I love you, Al'iro."

A gorgeous smile lights his face. "Say it again."

I smile against his lips. "I love you."

He drops his forehead to mine as his golden eyes search my own. "I know in my heart you are mine, Violet. I do not need my wings to glow to tell me this. Even if they never did, I would still want you as mine. Tell me, my Al'essa, do you choose me?"

"Yes."

CHAPTER 26

VIOLET

He captures my mouth in a claiming kiss and rolls me beneath him. His tongue curls around mine, deepening our kiss.

A soft moan escapes me as he cups one breast and brushes his thumb over the sensitive peak until it stiffens into a hardened bead.

He groans as I wrap my legs around him. With nothing between us, his manhood presses insistently against my inner thigh, hard and erect and so close to where I want him to be.

He rips his mouth from mine and stares down at me. His pupils blown wide so that only a thin rim of gold is visible around the edges. "I can scent your need, my Al'essa. Tell me... do you want me?"

I cup the back of his neck and pull his lips back down to mine as I whisper against them. "Yes."

He crushes his mouth to my own, his tongue finding

mine, curling around it and deepening our kiss. "You are mine," he breathes into my mouth. "My Al'essa."

Warmth pools deep inside me at his words. He presses a series of suctioning kisses along my jaw and down my neck. He closes his mouth over my left breast, swirling his tongue across the sensitive peak.

I gasp and arch up beneath him as he begins a gentle suction that drives my desire even higher.

I trace my hands over the thick cords of muscle lining his abdomen and chest. As I move my hands lower, he pulls back and his head snaps up to mine. "I want only to pleasure you," he whispers. "You do not need to—"

"I want to see you."

He pulls back just enough and my jaw drops as I get my first look at him. He's so big, I wonder if we'll fit.

"My lvost is similar to a Terran's, but—"

He stops as my fingers trace lightly over the several small bumps lining his shaft. A smaller tube extends from the tip of his crown and brushes against my finger. Thick liquid beads on the end, shimmering beneath the reflection of the light in our cavern. "What is this?"

"The tip enters the female's womb during the seeding."

"Seeding?"

"During our climax, the males of my kind release—"

I lower my gaze as my face heats even more. "I know what a climax is… It's just that males of my kind do not have a stem."

His brows furrow slightly. "Does it bother you?"

"No." I press a tender kiss to his lips to reassure him. "It's just different."

He kisses me again. "We do not have to do anything you do not wish, Violet."

"Can we just touch then? Until… I'm ready to do more?"

He nods, and I lean in and brush my mouth to his. Our kiss starts out slow and tender at first, but it quickly becomes something more urgent and full of need.

His heart pounds against mine as he pins me beneath him. Instead of feeling afraid, however, I love the feel of his weight over me.

He rips his mouth from mine and moves down my body. His hands glide up my thighs and gently parts them, opening me to his gaze. His golden eyes flick up to mine. "May I taste you?"

Breathless with anticipation, I nod.

He dips his head between my thighs, and I gasp as he drags his tongue through my already slick folds. When he reaches the apex at the top, a soft moan escapes me.

I thread my fingers through his hair, holding him in place. "Right there," I breathe. "That feels so good."

He growls low in arousal and concentrates his attention to the small bundle of nerves that make my entire body light up with pleasure.

I dig my heels into his shoulders as he continues to lave his tongue across the sensitive pearl of flesh.

Pleasure coils tight in my core. I've touched myself before but it's never felt this amazing. I run my fingers through his hair as sensation moves through me.

"Al'iro," I moan. "It's too much. I'm going to—"

"I want to bring you to release," he whispers. "I want you to flood my tongue with your nectar."

He continues to tease his tongue across the softly hooded flesh at the apex of my thighs. Carefully, he slides one finger inside me, and I gasp at the pleasurable sensation.

"Tell me how to touch you, my Al'essa."

I quickly realize he doesn't need any instruction as he slips another finger in my channel and heat pools deep in my core as he pumps them in and out of me. I arch up against him.

My entire body goes taut like a bowstring and then I'm coming harder than I ever have before. I cry out his name as wave after wave of pleasure washes over and through me.

He moves back up my body and his gaze holds mine, full of fire and possession.

I'm breathless and panting beneath him, and completely sated. He removes his fingers and brings them to his mouth. Closing his lips around them, he groans as if I'm the best thing he's ever tasted.

I glance down at his lvost, still hard and erect. "What about you? You didn't—"

He kisses me long and deep. "I want the first time I release to be when I'm inside you, my Al'essa. When I claim you, it will be in the way of my people. I will take you in the mating flight after our bonding ceremony."

He settles in the furs beside me and wraps me up in his arms and wings. He gently skims the tip of his nose alongside mine and whispers. "Tell me again that you choose me, Violet."

"I choose you, Al'iro. I choose you, my love."

He runs his fingers through my long chestnut hair. "I am sorry I have so little to offer you on this world."

I shake my head. "What are you talking about?"

"If we were on Aerilon, I would be able to give you the finest home and everything you could possibly desire. Jewels and precious metals and—"

I press a finger to his lips to silence him. "I don't need any of that to be happy, Al'iro. I only need you."

He drops his forehead gently to mine, then presses a tender kiss to my lips as he whispers, "You will always have me. I have been yours from the start, my Al'essa, and forever yours I will remain."

Curled up in his arms, I drift away to sleep. And as he holds me close, with his arms and wings wrapped tightly around me, I've never felt so safe and warm and completely and irrevocably loved beyond measure.

CHAPTER 27

AL'IRO

As I hold her close, I send a silent prayer to the Creator, thanking him for sparing her life. I close my eyes, as the image of her falling over the cliff fills my mind. It was the most terrifying moment of my existence.

When I saw her go over the side with the snowcat, my heart froze in my chest. In my time on the Defense Force, and during my enslavement, I have seen and endured many things. I thought I understood what true fear was, but I realize, now, I did not.

For when her eyes locked with mine a moment, just before tumbling over the edge, I have never been more afraid in my entire life. She is my Al'essa. I do not need my wings to glow to tell me this. It is a knowing deep in my soul.

She rests her head against my chest, and I am honored again by the amount of trust she places in me. I am thankful beyond measure that she knows I would never hurt or take advantage of her.

"You're like a furnace," she says, pulling me back from my thoughts.

I still, concerned. "Am I too warm?"

A soft laugh escapes her. "No, you feel wonderful." She tips her face up to mine, and a smile tugs at her lips. "I was going to ask if we could stay like this for a while longer. I don't think I'm quite ready to face the cold again just yet."

"Then, we will stay for a bit."

I do not mind in the slightest. I love the feel of her in my arms as she rests against me.

Fierce protectiveness fills me as I search beyond the entrance of the cave for any signs of danger. I will not be caught off-guard. Not when it comes to her. I nearly lost her, and I vow I will die before allowing any further harm to come to her.

A lone howl sounds in the distance, and worry fills me.

"What was that?" she asks.

My nostrils flare as I scent the wind. "A Lycaon. We must get dressed. They are close."

CHAPTER 28

VIOLET

We dress quickly. Al'iro stands and pulls me behind him as he stares out the cavern entrance.

A chorus of howls fills the air. "They will not hurt you," he says.

Worry ripples through me as I recognize what he doesn't voice aloud. They may not harm me, but he's not sure they will not hurt him.

Two glowing, yellow eyes blink at us from beneath the dark forest canopy. "Dakor?" Al'iro calls out. "Is that you?"

"Yes," a deep voice rumbles in reply.

My mouth drifts open as the wolf comes into view. His body several times larger than any wolf on Terra. With a thick, brown coat, his piercing yellow eyes lock on to mine. He shifts into a two-legged form in an instant.

I recognize him immediately. He's the same one I thought was going to eat us in the woods not long ago.

This time, however, he is completely unclothed. He has a long vertical line in his skin where male anatomy should be.

He looks at Al'iro. "Luken disappeared shortly after we saw you last. He went after the Terran female who was injured in the woods."

I inhale sharply. "Are you talking about Elain? The one I was with when—"

He nods. "She was heavily injured. After we chased one A'kai away and killed the other, Luken—our Alpha—went searching for her."

"How is this possible? She was injured... she thought she was dying."

"She suffered heavy blood loss. He was following her trail, but a storm came, separating us." He lowers his gaze. "We are still searching for them."

Hope fills me. "You're sure she was alive?"

"Yes, we are certain."

Tears sting my eyes, but I blink them back. I tip up my chin as I meet his gaze evenly. "My name is Violet. Please... when you find them, will you tell her I'm okay?"

He nods.

Al'iro steps forward. "You can bring her to our territory. We can keep her safe behind our force shield."

Dakor's expression darkens. "Do you believe our pack to be weak? Do you doubt our ability to keep her safe?"

"No." Al'iro sighs. "Must everything be about strength and weakness to your people?"

A snarl curls Dakor's lips, and Al'iro pulls me behind him to shield me.

I'm worried for him, however, so I step out and to his side, taking his hand. I level a dark glare at Dakor. "Do not threaten us," I grind out, trying to sound more brave than I feel right now.

His brows draw together as his gaze darts to Al'iro, then back to me. "I would never harm you, Violet."

I keep my eyes locked on his as I stand next to Al'iro.

"Are all Terran females this fierce?" A low growl rumbles his chest, his glowing eyes fixing me with a piercing stare. "Or do you mean to initiate the mating challenge?"

Al'iro's lips pull back in a snarl, baring his fangs. "She is mine," he grinds out.

The way he says this sends a shiver down my spine, not one of fear, but of something else entirely. My whole body flushes with warmth when he curls an arm around my waist and pulls me close.

I'm surprised when Dakor straightens, then dips his chin in a subtle acknowledgement. "Forgive me. I did not realize."

"Why are you here?" Al'iro asks.

"I came to warn you. Our pack killed an A'kai a few hours ago, at the edge of our territory. We have detected no others, but where there is one, there may be more."

Relief moves through me. Maybe the one they killed was the same one hunting us.

As if sensing my thoughts, Al'iro darts a knowing glance at me before returning his attention to Dakor. "I suspect the one you killed was the same one hunting us."

"Good," Dakor replies. "We are still searching for Luken and the Terran female, but we will remain vigilant. I suggest you do the same." He pauses. "If you find yourself in need of aid, call out to us. Whichever of us is nearby will respond and help you."

"Thank you," Al'iro says, the hard edge to his tone completely gone now.

Out of habit, I extend my hand.

Al'iro goes completely still, and Dakor hesitates; his eyes shift warily to Al'iro before he finally takes my hand. "Thank you for searching for my friend and my people."

Gently, he squeezes my hand. "We will continue our efforts and will not stop until we have freed all of them from the A'kai." He releases my hand and steps back.

His gaze drifts to Al'iro's wings, his expression turning grave. "Your wings... are they repairable?"

Al'iro nods. "Yes, but not without the proper equipment and another Healer to set them." Dakor opens his mouth, but Al'iro adds, "A Healer with a history of treating broken wings."

"If I could, I would help you," Dakor says. "But yours would be the first wing injury I have ever treated. And I do not wish to risk causing further damage."

A distant howl draws his attention, and I watch in wonder as he shifts into his wolf form. His yellow eyes hold mine a moment before he turns and races back into the forest.

CHAPTER 29

AL'IRO

Fierce possessiveness fills me as I hold Violet close to my side. I watch in satisfaction as Dakor retreats back into the woods. I wanted to rip off his arm when he took Violet's hand.

Violet is mine. How dare he touch her.

And yet, she is the one who initiated the contact.

I have seen Alana and Harry do this before—the standard Terran gesture of greeting and parting. Even so, bitter jealousy rose within me as Dakor took her hand. He found her desirable, and seemed delighted when he thought she was trying to initiate the mating challenge.

I have heard of the Lycaon mating challenge. It sounds as barbaric as the mating battle of the Mosaurans. The Lycaons and Mosaurans fight their potential mates, and if they win, the female accepts them as hers and they become a mated pair.

My eyes slide to Violet. She should not be conquered. She should be worshipped.

Myriad thoughts flood my mind as I lead her back into the cave.

"Are we safe here?" she asks, and I hate the anxious look in her eyes. I desperately wish I could fly. If I could, we would already be back at my ship, and she would no longer have to be afraid.

"It would be best to be higher up. It would give us more warning if someone approaches." I meet her gaze evenly. "Wait here. I will check the cliff wall for other caverns."

I start to leave, but her small hand on my forearm stops me abruptly. Her hazel eyes stare up at me, full of concern. "Be careful."

"I will. I will return soon."

As I leave the cave, I cannot still the fear in my heart at leaving her behind. I pray the Lycaons ended the life of the A'kai who was tracking us—and I have no doubt that he was. He would not so easily give up a steady food source. Not on a planet as stark as this.

My thoughts turn again to Violet's friend. I hope Luken found her alive. Even if he is Lycaon, I know now for certain that he will not harm her.

I extend my claws and begin scaling the cliff wall. I will find a safe shelter for us tonight. One that is more easily defendable than the one we're in now. I have to. My Al'essa needs rest.

We still have a long journey before us, and she'll need all her strength.

CHAPTER 30

VIOLET

Worry tightens my chest as I wait for Al'iro to return. I should have gone with him. I know he wants to keep me safe, but I'm afraid for him. As strong as he is, it's still dangerous.

I remain completely still and alert as minutes tick by like an eternity. A small shiver runs through me, both from fear and the cold. I was reluctant to leave the safety and warmth of his arms, but I know he's right. We have to find a more secure shelter. Especially if we're going to be here overnight.

Another howl sounds in the distance, and a chill runs down my spine. I know the Lycaons are on our side, but that doesn't mean they're not frightening. They remind me of werewolves. Watching Dakor transform was a jarring experience.

After all I've been through, ever since I woke up in a cage, I'd thought I had seen everything, but it seems I was wrong. Apparently, there are dragon men, vampire-elvish men, werewolves, and—I think on Al'iro's people—the Fae are real, as well.

A faint scraping of stone draws my attention, followed by several small rocks falling just outside the cave entrance.

A large shadow drops to the ground, and I cry out a moment before I realize it's Al'iro.

"Violet, it is me."

My heart hammers in my chest as I practically collapse back against the wall, relieved that it's him.

He takes my hand. "Forgive me. I did not mean to scare you. I should have announced myself. I forget your species cannot see as well in the dark as mine."

I give him a faint smile. "It's all right. I'm just glad you're back."

His expression is troubled. "I would never abandon you."

I realize he says this because he remembers my story about my father leaving my mother, and how I always worried a man would do the same to me. He cups my chin. "I am yours, Violet. And I will remain so until the Creator comes to take me from this world to the next."

My heart clenches. I stretch up on my toes and press a kiss to his lips. "I'm not worried about you leaving me, my love. I'm worried about *you* getting hurt."

His expression softens. "And I worry for *you*."

"You found us a new shelter?" I ask, hopeful.

A handsome smile curves his mouth. "I believe you will like it."

"Why?"

He arches a brow. "You will have to see for yourself." He holds out his arms. "Come, I will take you."

I step into his embrace, and he gently lifts me as I wrap my arms and legs around his front. Clinging to his front like this, I can feel the pounding of his heart against my chest.

The powerful muscles of his body flex against mine as he climbs the cliff wall.

When we reach a cave entrance high up the side, he carefully lowers my feet to the floor. I bite back my disappointment when he steps back; I already miss the feel of his body against mine. "Wait here," he says. "I will go retrieve our belongings."

I nod and watch him scale back down the wall.

When he finally reaches the bottom, he disappears into our old cave.

A flash of light in the darkness catches my eyes. I turn toward it as a pair of red, glowing orbs blink and then disappear. I frown as I study the area, searching for it again, but see nothing.

As I glance down, I see Al'iro already ascending the cliff face wall. He pulls himself into our new cave, and I touch his arm, whispering quietly. "Something is out there."

He spins toward the forest, his gaze searching the dense forest beyond the falls. "What did you see?"

"It looked like a pair of glowing, red eyes."

"There are many predators on this planet. Most of them are nocturnal."

Nightmarish images fill my mind at his words. He turns toward me, cupping my cheek. "You need not worry. We are safer up here. I will be able to detect if anything comes near us."

It's dark outside, but there is just enough light from the moon that I'm able to see inside the cavern. The ceiling is almost a full head taller than Al'iro, and there is plenty of space to move around. It is also pleasantly warm in here. "It feels warmer than our other cave." I place my hand on the wall and feel the heat coming from the stone.

"Come." Al'iro smiles. "I have found something I think you will like."

I follow him toward the back, and my mouth drifts open when I notice a large pool of water with steam rising from the surface. "Many of the caves on this world seem to have these warm springs. We have a few cavern outposts we chose because of these pools of heated water."

A wide smile splits my face. "This is wonderful." I'm already imagining a nice warm soak.

As I study the water, I notice instead of just one pool, there are actually two. One is slightly elevated and beside the other. It is a bit smaller and spills over into the larger second one.

"We can use one for drinking and another for bathing," I tell him.

"Yes. I'll keep watch while you bathe."

Without another word, he walks to the front of the cave, leaving his back to me.

I wonder why he does this. It's not as if he hasn't already seen me naked. My cheeks heat as I think on what we did earlier.

Carefully, I peel out of my many layers of clothing. When I enter the water, a sigh of contentment escapes my lips. The tense muscles of my neck and shoulders relax at the embrace of the soothing warmth.

I look toward Al'iro. The silver moonlight highlights his heavily muscled form, lending him an ethereal appearance. He is complete and utter masculine perfection, too perfect to be real.

I dip my head beneath the water to wash my hair, and when I climb out of the pool and wrap myself in one of the furs, I call out to him. "You can turn around now."

"No," he says in a low voice.

My head jerks back. "Why not?"

"I do not want to see you."

Worry tightens my chest. Has he changed his mind about me? Suddenly, decided he doesn't want me after all?

It doesn't make any sense.

He spins toward me. "What is this emotion? Why are you worried?"

"I—" I stop, not sure what to say. "Did you change your mind about us?"

Unable to stop myself, I move closer to him and reach out to brush my fingers across his soft, warm mouth. A question sits on the tip of my tongue, and I'm hesitant to ask, but I know I have to. I need an answer before this goes any further. "Why do you want me? Is it because of the bond?"

"Yes," he replies, without hesitation and my heart sinks. I lower my gaze.

He cups my chin, lifting my face back up to his. "But, it is more than that," he continues. "It is who you are, Violet."

"What do you mean?"

"You are everything I could ever want in a partner. You are intelligent, beautiful, and strong."

"I'm not strong," I tell him. "I—"

"Strength is not only a physical attribute. It is something that comes from in here." He places his hand to my chest, directly over my beating heart. "It is a part of your very soul." His golden eyes search mine. "You survived unimaginable horrors, and, yet... you not only survived them, but you refused to let them break you."

He presses a tender kiss to my lips. "I love you, Violet. You are mine, my Al'essa, and I will never change my mind about us."

He pulls me close, wrapping me up in the comfort and shelter of his wings.

A low howl sounds outside, and we both still. Al'iro's eyes snap toward the cave entrance and he moves toward it, scanning the forest.

He turns toward me. "We must go."

"What? Why?"

The question has barely left my mouth when I hear the sound of stones scraping against each other.

"Why are you here?" Al'iro asks. Ice-cold fear floods my veins when I realize he is talking to someone I cannot see. "We already talked with you earlier. Why have you returned so soon?"

"There are several A'kai in these woods." I recognize Dakor's voice. "The others report at least four."

Al'iro stills and it is easy to see the worry in his expression.

Dakor continues. "I have come to retrieve you. To offer you shelter within our camp."

Al'iro bristles. "She is mine," he growls.

Dakor puts up his hands as he stands just inside the cave entrance. "I recognize your claim. I will not challenge you for the female."

If we were on Terra, I'd be appalled at all this talk of challenge and claim. But they're aliens. I cannot judge them according to my culture.

Please," Dakor adds. "Four A'kai is too many for you to protect her from on your own."

Al'iro darts a glance at me, then turns back to Dakor. "We will take you up on your offer."

Dakor hands me a blaster. "Do you know how to use this?"

I nod and tuck it into my clothing.

Al'iro quickly helps me secure our belongings and puts an extra fur over the layers I already have on, carefully tightening a makeshift belt around them, until I'm so puffed up with fur, I practically have to waddle to his side.

He frowns. "Are you all right? Why are you walking like this?"

"Because I feel like a giant snowball."

Dakor laughs, revealing two rows of sharp fangs. I'm not afraid, though. He's not the enemy. The A'kai are.

"How far away is your camp?" Al'iro asks.

"Not far," Dakor replies. "But, we must hurry." His nostrils flare. "The A'kai are close. Their scent is growing stronger on the wind."

Al'iro tips up his chin, scenting the air. His eyes widen slightly, and he gathers me in his arms. "Hold tightly to me. We must move quickly."

CHAPTER 31

AL'IRO

Violet wraps her arms and legs around my front, holding on to me as we descend the cliff face and race through the woods. Dakor is fast. His speed nearly matching that of the V'loryns and the A'kai, but somehow I manage to keep up.

A cold wind blows through the forest and panic tightens my chest at the scent of the A'kai growing even stronger.

As if sensing this, Dakor glances over his shoulder. "Hurry. We must make it to my pack. They will not dare attack with all of us there."

I follow him through the woods and across the snow-covered terrain. Silver moonlight filters through the trees, casting sinister shadows in its wake as we pass. Violet's heart pounds against mine, and the acrid smell of her fear permeates the air so thick it is almost cloying.

I tip my head up and catch another scent—one of several Lycaons up ahead. "We're almost there," I whisper in her ear as we continue to run, trying to reassure her.

Her entire body begins trembling. Before I can ask what is wrong, she pulls the blaster from her belt and fires it over my shoulder.

A thunderous roar pierces the air, and I glance over my shoulder at the A'kai racing behind us, chasing us through the forest.

The wound on his chest is visible as he continues his pursuit.

She aims again, but misses.

"Give me the Terran!" he yells. "Now!"

"No!"

Dakor spins. "Go! I will hold him off!"

He charges toward the A'kai, and I turn just as they clash in a tangled mess of fangs and claws.

Out of the corner of my eye, something lunges toward me. I spin as Violet cries out.

Lightning fast, another A'kai wraps an arm around her waist, knocking me off balance, causing me to stumble to the side as he tries to pull her away.

I slash at him with my claws, and he cries out, relinquishing his grip on my Al'essa.

Anger floods my system as he charges toward us again.

Without hesitation, I pull her behind me, taking the brunt of his attack. He slams into me, sending us sprawling backward and into the snow. I sink my teeth into his shoulder, and he jerks away.

I kick at him, but he rushes me again, his eyes a feral black, and as we fight, he bares his fangs even as his movements begin to slow as my venom takes effect.

Movement behind me catches me off guard, and I spin just as another A'kai lunges at me, sinking his teeth deep into my neck.

A blast of light arcs toward him, and he roars in pain as it hits his back. He stills and falls to one side, dead in the snow.

I jerk my head toward Violet as she aims the blaster at the second one and hits him.

My limbs are heavy and uncoordinated as I struggle to stand. Using the last of my strength, I rush toward the one fighting with Dakor and slash my claws across his throat.

The A'kai slumps forward, going still as obsidian blood pools beneath him.

"Thanks, I—" Dakor stops. His brow furrows deeply as he looks at my neck. "You were bitten?"

I manage to nod as I drop to my knees in the snow before falling back.

Violet kneels beside me, cupping my cheek, as she stares down at me in panic. "Al'iro, what's wrong?"

"A'kai venom," I rasp. "It is toxic to my people."

My gaze slides to Dakor at her side. "You must keep her safe."

"No," an anguished cry escapes her. "Please, don't die. I lo—"

My eyes roll up in the back of my head, and I fall away into oblivion.

CHAPTER 32

VIOLET

His eyes close, and he falls still. An anguished cry escapes me as I wrap my arms around him, burying my face in his chest, sobs wracking through me. "No!"

A warm hand on my shoulder pulls gently at me, but I shove it away, refusing to leave Al'iro. "Don't touch me!"

It lifts away. A moment later, Dakor's voice speaks softly overhead. "He will be well, Violet. I promise you. It is simply the venom. His body must process it. Then, he will awaken."

I draw in a shaking breath and lift my gaze to him. "He's not going to die?"

"No." He gives me a faint smile. "He will live."

His head jerks to the left and my heart stops. "What is it?"

"We must go," he whispers urgently. "Quickly."

I stand and watch as he lifts Al'iro, carrying him over his shoulder. He groans as if Al'iro's weight is a heavy burden for him, but moves swiftly anyway, and we make our way through the woods.

Movement catches my eye, and I cry out as something catches me around the waist. I'm lifted into the air and against a heavily muscled and bare chest. Glowing, orange eyes meet mine. "I mean you no harm, but we must hurry," the Lycaon's deep voice rumbles above me. "There are more A'kai in these woods, and we must make it back to our camp."

Still startled, I blink up at him.

"I am Ryken," he says. "You are safe with us."

Trees move past us in a blur as we race through the woods. I keep my gaze trained on the surrounding forest, searching for any sign of the A'kai and praying we can outrun them.

Up ahead, bright light glows in the distance. As we draw closer, I realize it is a fire near the entrance to a cave.

"Lower the shield!" Ryken calls out.

A high-pitched howl answers as we race toward it.

"What is—"

"Do not fear," Ryken says. "It is my pack."

A moment later, we enter a cave mouth, barely skirting the ring of fire lining the entrance in the process. My eyes widen as Ryken carefully sets me down on my feet.

My gaze travels over the cavern. The ceiling is much taller than the cave Al'iro and I took shelter in and several times as wide. I notice openings around the main space covered with patchwork curtains of hanging white furs.

Private rooms, perhaps.

It's pleasantly warm in here, thanks to the fire, and the ceiling slopes up toward the entrance, allowing the smoke to escape rather than remain trapped inside. I notice makeshift racks of stretched hides and white furs, along with slabs of meat, smoking near the flames.

Five enormous wolves stalk toward us, their coats varying shades of brown and silver.

One of them turns his glowing yellow eyes to me, and his nostrils flare. His gaze flashes to Al'iro, and a low growl issues from his chest as Dakor sets him on a pile of white furs.

Without hesitation, I step between the wolf and Al'iro and level an icy glare at him, mustering all of my courage.

The wolf shifts instantly into his two-legged form. "We will not harm your mate."

"Thank you."

He dips his chin in subtle acknowledgment. "You are welcome."

My gaze darts to the front of the cave. "Are you sure fire will keep the A'kai away?"

A slight grin tips his mouth. "We have a force shield to protect us. But, if it goes down, the fire will alert us if they try to get in. It is a... secondary precaution. Those *maltaks* may believe they are invincible, but they burn just like everything else."

CHAPTER 33

VIOLET

"**A**re you hungry?" Ryken asks.

"Thank you, but I'm fine."

"We are still searching for your friend. Our Alpha, Luken, went looking for her, but they still have not returned to us."

I blink back tears as I think of Elain.

I should have ignored her when she told me to leave. I should have stayed with her and tried to protect her.

"You may have this room," Dakor says, interrupting my thoughts. He gestures to one of the openings covered by a fur patchwork curtain. "For you and your mate."

I thank him as he and Ryken carry Al'iro into the space. It's not large, but it isn't small, either—just enough room for a pallet of soft furs in one corner and a few shelves carved out along the opposite wall for belongings.

The light from the fire casts just enough illumination that I can see clearly, but when Dakor places a few crystals along one of the shelves, the space grows even brighter.

"L'sair crystals…. They will add extra lighting and warmth."

"Thank you."

I kneel beside Al'iro and cover him with one of the furs. "How long do you think it will be before he wakes up?"

Dakor shakes his head. "I am uncertain. Perhaps a few hours, maybe less." He kneels beside me until his face is even with mine. "Do not worry. We will look after you both."

While his words sound sincere, I'm still worried about Al'iro. The sooner we get him back to his people, and a Healer who can treat his wings, the better. "Can you get word to his people?"

"No. Unfortunately, this area is lined with some sort of ore that makes communications difficult. It does not affect our shield however." He pauses, his piercing gaze studying me a moment, and his nostrils flare. He narrows his eyes. "You do not carry the Aerilon's scent."

I blink up at him. "What do you mean?"

"You are not fully mated to him."

My cheeks flare with heat as he continues. "We will watch over Al'iro, but once he awakens, you do not have to go with him."

I blink several times. "Why wouldn't I go with him?"

"He cannot keep you safe," Dakor states. "It is obvious his wings are injured. And when we fought the A'kai, he fell."

I bristle. "It could have just as easily happened to you."

His expression hardens. "Our pack is strong. We can protect you better than he can."

"Look, Dakor, I appreciate your help and your concern, but I'm not leaving him. Where he goes, so do I."

He shares a glance with Ryken, and something about it unsettles me. "We will leave you to rest. Please, consider our offer to stay here until our Alpha comes back with the Terran female. I do not doubt they live and will return soon."

He has a lot of faith in Luken. I only pray it isn't unfounded. Elain was injured; her life depends upon it.

When they leave, I settle next to Al'iro. Something about the Lycaon's expressions makes me nervous, but I don't know why. They've been nothing but kind and helpful to us so far, but I cannot still the nagging concern lingering in the back of my mind.

Shifting toward Al'iro, I cup his cheek, turning his face in my direction. "Please, wake up," I whisper. "I know they said you'll be fine, but I'm worried. I miss your voice and your smile. Please be all right."

A few hours pass before Dakor enters the room again, his expression soft as he studies me. "He will be fine. I promise."

"Thanks."

"Tell me, Violet, how many of your people are missing?"

I open my mouth to speak, but Al'iro shifts slightly, drawing my attention to him.

CHAPTER 34

AL'IRO

The scent of smoke fills my nostrils. My eyes snap open, and I jerk up in the bed.

"Al'iro?" Violet's soft voice calls beside me.

I turn to find her kneeling next to me on a pile of furs. I swiftly scan the space, noting a hanging curtain made of fur covering the cave exit. "Where are we?"

Before she can answer, another smell floods my system, and a growl rumbles from deep within. "Lycaons. There are several of them," I whisper. "Where—"

Dakor moves in the corner, catching my eye. "You are in our cave. We brought you here to recover after you were bitten by the A'kai."

I shakily push myself up to standing, placing my hand on the wall to steady myself. Violet stands with me and takes my hand. "How are you feeling?"

"My limbs still feel a bit heavy, but otherwise, I am fine."

She smiles. "Thank goodness."

Dakor's eyes travel over me in assessment. He is a Healer

among his people, like myself. "The venom should be completely out of your system within half a day."

Ryken steps into the room next to him, and I note the way his gaze locks on to Violet. Fierce possessiveness overtakes me, and I curl an arm around her waist, tugging her to my side.

Something dark and primal unfurls deep within me as she accepts this possessive gesture and wraps her arm around my waist, in return.

"Thank you for aiding us, Dakor. We will be on our way as soon as my strength returns."

Dakor frowns. "It would be unwise to travel at night. You know this. There could be more A'kai out there."

As anxious as I am to return to my people, I know he is right. "We will wait until first light, then."

He dips his chin in affirmation, his gaze sliding to Violet. "How many Terran females are out there?"

"I'm not sure," she answers. "There were at least twenty of us kept in the same cargo bay, but there were more throughout the rest of the ship. I don't know how many."

I look at him, adding what I've learned from Alana and Harry. "The other Terrans we have encountered all say the same. The problem is… there were just as many A'kai, if not more, who came down to the planet's surface when they evacuated their ship."

Dakor clenches his jaw. "No wonder there have been so many of them in our territory lately."

"What of the other A'kai—the ones who have been trapped here with us for these past five cycles? Have you seen them in the woods? Or are they keeping to their territory?"

"It seems they are keeping to their territory. For now," Ryken answers. "But, that could soon change, now that the addition of their brethren tips the numbers in their favor."

I curl my wing around Violet, subconsciously wanting to

shield her from danger. "We need to get back to my people and behind their shield."

"We have a shield," Dakor says. "It would be safer for you to remain here."

"I have to get back. I am one of only a few Healers among the Aerilon. I cannot abandon them."

"Then, you should leave Violet here, where she will be safe."

"She will be safe with *us*."

"But, not with *you*," he counters. "You are injured. You cannot expect to be able to protect her in your current state."

Violet tips up her chin. "I'm not entirely defenseless. I have a blaster, and I've had training. I—"

"You are small," Dakor interrupts her. "Smaller than any of our people, or the A'kai, thus, easily subdued. You will stay here with us. We will keep you safe."

She narrows her eyes. "I'm going with Al'iro."

"No. You are not," Ryken says.

She levels a dark glare at them. "I did not escape one captor only to be kept by another," she grinds out. "I will not be caged. Ever again."

He blinks several times. "You believe we wish to imprison you? Keep you as a slave?"

"If I'm not allowed to leave of my own free will, how else am I supposed to consider this?" she asks, her hazel eyes locked on to his in challenge.

"We do not mean to keep you as a slave. We merely wish to protect you."

They stare at one another in charged silence, tension hanging thick in the air. I pull her closer into my side as a warning growl builds in my chest.

His glowing, orange eyes dilate until only a thin rim of color remains around the edges. "You should know that to lock eyes with a male of my species in this way is considered an initiation of the mating challenge." He takes a small step closer to her, his nostrils flaring. "If this is your intent, I accept."

My lips curl back, and I bare my fangs. "She. Is. Mine."

"I am his," she states firmly, "and he is my mate. You *will not* keep me from him."

I want to roar my happiness to the stars at her declaration of claiming.

Dakor lowers his eyes and gives her a subtle nod. "I respect your choice. But I must insist that you remain with us. For your own good."

"Why is that?"

"Because his people"—he gestures to me—"are allied with and live with the V'loryns. The V'loryns are like the A'kai—able to manipulate the mind of another through the simple act of touch."

The acrid scent of Violet's fear floods the room. "Is this true?"

"Yes," I answer honestly. "But, they are not like the A'kai. They would never—"

"They are deceitful, just like the A'kai," Dakor continues. "They took a Terran female—one of your kin. He claimed her as his mate, and we do not know if it was done of her own free will."

Violet's gaze turns to me, full of concern. "Is he talking about Alana?"

I grip her shoulders and meet her gaze evenly. "I promise you that Commander Vorek is a good male. He is V'loryn, and he is my friend. He would never violate the mind of another. He loves Alana, and she, him. I have seen it with my own eyes."

Violet's brows draw together in a contemplative look before she finally nods. "I believe you," she whispers.

"You are making a mistake," Dakor grumbles.

"No, she is not," I snap. "It is *you* who are wrong. The V'loryns are nothing like the A'kai. They are good."

"Tell that to my brethren who are constantly harassed by their people, looked down upon as if we were common criminals when we go anywhere near their planetary system," he grinds out.

"Do you blame them? When you harbor this same level of mistrust toward their people as well? Comparing them to the A'kai?" I huff out a frustrated breath. "The A'kai are their enemies, too. Or did you conveniently forget that?"

"You are a fool to trust them." He narrows his eyes, studying me. "But, perhaps, it is something else. Maybe they have manipulated *your* mind. Did you ever stop to consider this?"

Sighing heavily in frustration, I shake my head. "It is a crime punishable by death for one of their people to violate the mind of another."

"That such a law was made among their people, suggests it has been violated many times," he says darkly.

Violet moves between us. "Stop arguing," she snaps. "This isn't doing anyone any good."

Ryken and Dakor blink several times, seemingly stunned she would stand before them unafraid—despite her smaller size—and demand they listen to her.

Their expressions quickly shift into what I recognize as desire. Female Lycaons are known for their fierceness. A quality they obviously see in Violet, judging by the way they gaze at her.

I pull her back to my side, glaring at them both. "I already told you. She. Is. Mine. She has chosen me. We leave tomorrow at dawn, and you will not stop us."

Dakor runs a hand roughly through his hair. "She is a life giver. What you do is dangerous. Do you not realize this?"

"I firmly believe she will be safer with *my* people, behind *our* force shield, and on *our* ship that still functions despite being grounded."

"You are a fool," Dakor practically spits. "But, we will escort you as far as we can and see you safely toward your ship." He looks at her again. "If you change your mind, you are welcome to stay with us. Please... I ask that you take this night to consider our offer."

She tips up her head and takes my hand. "I've already made my decision."

When they leave, we settle back in the bed. Dark and primal instincts unfurl from deep within me. The mere scent of the Lycaons nearby fills me with fierce possessiveness.

I carefully pull the soft furs over her to keep her warm. I wrap my arms and wings around her, holding her close.

She lifts her head to me. "What if the Lycaons try to stop me from leaving tomorrow?"

"Let them try," I growl. "You are mine. Not theirs."

CHAPTER 35

AL'IRO

When morning comes, part of me dreads knowing we must leave this shelter because the A'kai are still out there. But I am eager to return to my people.

As safe as the Lycaons believe their cave is, I know for a fact our ship and its force shield are even safer. Not to mention, there are technological amenities which make life much more bearable on this ice rock of a planet.

If we were to stay here, and Violet were ever harmed, I would have no access to superior healing tech like I do back on our ship.

When we step out of our room and into the main area of the cave, the Lycaons turn to us. As I scan the cavern, I cannot help but offer, "If you come with us, I will speak to Commander Vorek about allowing you to settle with our people. Everything on the ship still functions, except for the engines."

Dakor studies me a moment before speaking. "Such a

gesture must be decided upon by our Alpha, and Luken is still missing. When he returns, I will relay your offer to him, but I doubt he will agree."

"Why?"

Dakor's eyes dart to Violet. "You truly trust the V'loryns?"

"Without hesitation or doubt." I meet his gaze evenly. "We share a common enemy, Dakor. Together, we could push back the A'kai, despite the increase in their numbers."

With a slight clench of his jaw, he tips his head. "What you suggest would sound wise, if not for our unpleasant history with the V'loryns. But we are open to discussions about coordinating the search for the Terrans." He narrows his eyes. "Does Commander Vorek of the V'loryns speak for your people, now, since you have joined them?"

"No. But it is still his ship. He was... kind enough to extend the offer for us to stay with them. And we have."

He nods but says nothing. It does not escape me how the others keep looking at Violet. As much as they distrust the V'loryns, I understand it is difficult for them to accept that she chooses to come with me and to live among them.

"If you would but meet with Commander Vorek, you would see he is an honorable male," I tell them. "He is fully mated to the Terran female he rescued. He is good and kind to her, and despite the belief their people do not feel or express emotions, it is easy to see how much he loves her."

This must surprise them because they blink several times and exchange curious glances between one another.

I used to believe the V'loryns were uncaring and unfeeling automatons, but after meeting Vorek, I quickly realized this was not true. They simply hide their emotions, but they still have them.

Dakor stands. "Ryken and I will accompany you to the edge of the forest. But it will be a difficult journey beyond that. The scale of the falls is very steep and treacherous. It will slow our—"

"I may not have full use of my wings, but I am still able to glide on the wind," I explain. "If you will see us that far, I can manage the rest of the way. It is not far from the valley to the mountain pass and to my people."

Dakor studies Violet a moment. "You are certain you wish to leave?"

She moves closer to me and takes my hand. "Yes."

As we stand at the entrance of the cave, I carefully layer another fur tunic over the three Violet is already wearing. I tighten the belt around her to cinch it in place and carefully pull the hood up to cover her head.

Her luminous, hazel eyes meet mine, and a smile tips my lips when I realize they are green in the morning light.

My Al'essa is truly the most beautiful female I have ever seen.

I offer to carry her as we trudge through the snow, but she staunchly refuses, insisting she can walk. It is easy to see the admiration reflected behind Dakor's and Ryken's eyes as they watch her.

They must realize, as I have, that despite her smaller form, she is strong in other ways—her strength of will equal to that of either a Lycaon or Aerilon female.

Snow falls heavily all around us as the wind whips through the forest. The cold air claws at our forms as we make our way beneath the thick canopy of trees. Ryken walks ahead of us, while Dakor and I walk behind Violet.

Each of us is silent as we listen and watch for any signs we are being tracked. The A'kai are skilled hunters, able to move with lethal stealth and speed. Despite the cold and unpleasant weather, I am glad of the snowfall for it covers our tracks.

Dakor points up ahead. "We are nearly to the ridge."

With a slight tightening of my jaw, I mentally prepare myself for the searing pain I know will soon come. Each time I've had to use my wings to glide to safety, I feel an agony unlike any I have ever known. But as my gaze turns to Violet, I know I would change nothing. She is worth all I have gone through, and I would do it again, given the choice.

Now, I must simply make one more flight before we reach home. I welcome getting my wings repaired and, therefore, an end to this pain.

Dakor opens his mouth to speak, but stops abruptly. My heart stops as Ryken goes completely still up ahead.

I look to Dakor, his eyes wide and searching. "A'kai," he whispers.

As one, the three of us surround Violet, placing our backs to her as we scan the forest, each crouched in a defensive stance.

My pulse pounds in my ears, ice cold fear flooding my veins.

I have to protect Violet. I cannot allow them to take her.

"How many?" I ask the Lycaons, knowing their superior sense of smell probably tells them how many A'kai are in the woods.

"At least two," Dakor whispers in reply.

A threatening growl rumbles in my chest. "Violet is all that matters. Whatever happens, protect her."

"Agreed," Ryken replies.

A flash of movement catches my eye, and I turn just as the first A'kai lunges toward Dakor. In a blur of motion, he and Ryken shift into their beast forms.

They descend upon the A'kai, swiping out with their claws.

I join the fray, using my claws to rend flesh from bone as we pin him to the ground and tear into his flesh.

His glowing, green eyes burn with anger as he struggles to break free. But there are three of us and we have no intention of letting him go. Our fight must be to the death.

He dared to hunt my Al'essa. And now, I will be certain he hunts no more.

A blast of light races past me, crashing into a nearby tree.

Spinning to face it, the world shifts into slow motion as Violet jumps in front of me, shielding me from the attack.

A blast of light explodes behind her as she cries out in pain, collapsing to the snow in a crumpled heap.

"No!"

Blood pools beneath her body in the snow as I gather her in my arms. Pressing my hand to her gaping wound, I cover the burned and charred flesh surrounding the injury, trying to stem the bleeding.

Dakor and Ryken rush to the A'kai and attack.

He fires off another shot, and I spin away but too late as the blast hits my side.

"Take her!" Dakor yells. "Go!"

"Hurry!" Ryken yells.

Gritting my teeth against the pain, I gather her in my arms and run toward the ridgeline. If I can make it there, I can glide the rest of the way home, close enough my people should see us and be able to help.

My heart pounds as I race to the cliff. Only a few more steps and we'll be safe. "Hold on, Violet."

Her hazel eyes blink up at me as she struggles to stay conscious.

"Hold on," I tell her again. "Do not fall asleep."

"Trying," she whimpers.

Every step is hard won as I make my way to the ridge, the

powdered snow so thick, I sink to my ankle with each step, slowing me down.

Fear tightens my chest as a vicious growl sounds close behind us. I do not have to turn around to know an A'kai is on my heels, pursuing. Only a few more steps and I'll make the cliff. "Give us the Terran!" he snarls.

"Never!"

I extend my wings, blinding pain ripping through my back as I catch the wind and drop off the ledge.

The cool breeze catches my sails and lifts us into the air. I glance down at Violet, then cry out as something sharp grips my leg.

I look down at the A'kai's claws deep in my flesh. His wide eyes meet mine with genuine fear behind them as I struggle to free myself.

The forest is a sea of snow-covered trees below. If he falls now, it will be to his death.

I kick out, making contact with his face, but he refuses to let go.

An angry growl rips from his throat as I twist and spin through the air, trying to shake him free.

My back burns like fire as I struggle to keep my wings extended, despite the terrible pain. My entire body quakes with agony. Unable to keep them out any longer, they fold against my back and we begin a spiraling descent to the ground.

Just over the tree line, I can see the ship. Two Mosaurans circle overhead. I recognize the silver scales of Commander Markus right away. "Help us!"

CHAPTER 36

VIOLET

My eyes blink open and closed as pain burns through me like fire, oblivion beckoning me into its welcoming abyss with the promise of an end to the pain.

Al'iro kicks at the A'kai as we spiral toward the ground. His wings snap open, abruptly halting our descent as a painful cry rips from his throat.

"Help us!" he calls out.

A deafening roar answers his cry, shaking the very snow from the trees. I turn my head and watch as a real-life dragon flies toward us, its silver scales shimmering iridescent beneath the light, wings billowing out like great sails from its sides.

It blocks out the sun a moment before diving toward us. Opening its mouth, it releases a stream of flame at the A'kai.

A terrified scream rips from his throat as he releases his grip on Al'iro and falls away.

"Violet! Hold on!" Al'iro grinds out, flapping his wings to slow our descent.

But it isn't enough. He spins and his back hits the ground, taking the brunt of the impact.

The moment we land, we begin rolling to the side and down the face of the mountain, tumbling over snow and rock as we descend. Pain explodes across the back of my head as I slam into a rock, and the world goes dark.

CHAPTER 37

AL'IRO

Awareness slowly trickles back into my mind, and my eyes blink open to the bright, blinding light of the med bay. Alana and Vorek stand over me, along with Healer Siran of the Mosaurans.

I jerk up to sitting. "Where is Violet?"

"She is here, my friend," Vorek reassures me.

Siran leans over me, the Healer scanning me from head to toe. It is only now I realize my wings and back do not ache. As though sensing my question, he meets my gaze. "We were able to repair the damage to your wings."

My relief is short-lived as I glance over his shoulder to see Violet in the MRU, unconscious.

I throw my legs over the side of the bed and nearly stumble as I rush toward her. Vorek places a hand on my arm to steady me. His glowing green eyes meet mine. "Be careful, my friend. You were severely injured. You've been asleep for two days."

I blink several times. "Two days?"

He rakes a hand roughly through his dark hair. "Commander Markus saw you struggling with the A'kai. He—"

"He saved us," I finish his sentence, just as Commander Markus moves to my side. His silver-white scales shimmer beneath the bright lights of the med bay as his violet eyes meet mine. His wings are tucked close to his back, and he dips his chin in a subtle nod.

"I am glad I was able to help you," he says.

His Terran mate—Lara—moves to his side, and he wraps a possessive arm around her waist.

"I am glad you were nearby."

"We had only just arrived," he says. "My mate wanted to visit her friend, Alana. And... Healer Siran wanted to gather more information on Terran anatomy and physiology, to expand our medical database."

It is strange to see the Mosaurans here in our med bay. Our alliance with their people is only recent, due to the fact that Commander Markus and Vorek now both have Terran mates.

"I owe you a debt, Commander."

"You owe me nothing."

Glancing down at Violet's still form, I place my hand on the glass, as if I could somehow touch her. My heart clenches. She appears so vulnerable and still. Tears sting my eyes, but I blink them back. "Will she recover?" I ask, both fearful and anxious for the answer.

Healer Siran gives me a hesitant look. "We removed her tracker. The injury she sustained from the blaster fire was severe, but I am hopeful she will heal."

Devastation fills me. 'Hopeful'—the word escapes my lips in barely a whisper. I have worked in medicine long enough to know what such a statement means, and the weight of this knowledge threatens to crush me beneath it.

Siran moves closer. "With the information Alana has

provided us on Terran anatomy and physiology, we were able to program the MRU to function more effectively at repairing her injuries. So, I am hopeful that—"

"I understand," I cut him off, not wanting to hear his attempts at reassurance any longer. Instead of comforting me, they are doing the exact opposite. "I will sit with her while she heals."

Alana places her palm on the glass, staring down at Violet. "Thank you for rescuing her," she says softly.

Vorek steps forward and rests a hand on my shoulder. "You should rest, my friend. You are still recovering."

"Would you? If it were your mate—Alana—here, instead of Violet?" I ask, my tone a bit harsher than I'd intended.

"She is your Al'essa?" His eyes widen slightly. "But your wings. They do not glow."

"It does not matter," I tell him as sadness tightens my chest. "I know she is my Fated One. Please, do not ask me to rest or tell me I need to recover. And there will be time for questions later. I'm going to sit with her until she awakens."

He falls silent, then dips his chin in a subtle nod before stepping back. "If you need anything, Al'iro, I am here."

I give him a faint smile. For all his stoicism, it is easy to read the compassion in his eyes. He understands what I am going through. I've seen his love for Alana. V'loryns are not supposed to love or express emotion, but it is easy to read the depth of his emotions when he looks at his mate.

It has been two days since I woke up, and Violet is still in the MRU. I'm studying her read out when I hear the doors slide open behind me to the med bay.

"Good morning," Vorek says. "I—" He stops speaking abruptly.

I frown and turn to face him. "What is wrong?"

His brow furrows deeply. "Your wings."

I glance down at them, and my jaw falls slack when I notice they are glowing brightly. "I was right. She *is* my Al'essa. I knew it in my heart."

"Your fated one," Vorek speaks softly.

Emotions lodge in my throat, but I somehow manage to speak around them. "Yes."

I lift my gaze to the monitor, noting the same markings on her back as the other Terran females we've recovered from the A'kai so far.

The words 'Blood breeder' are carved across the flesh of all of them in A'kai glyphs. Anger roils within me and I turn to Vorek. "You told me, after you found Alana, you wanted to end the A'kai on this world. All of them." I clench my jaw. "At the time, I was... conflicted. I am a Healer, and it goes against my training to take life when I have been taught how to save it. But now... I understand." I pause, riding my emotions to the apex. "I understand—I agree with you. Completely. We cannot allow them to continue as they are. While the A'kai still live, they will always be a danger to the Terrans."

His gaze holds mine, but he says nothing. In his eyes, I recognize the same anger burning in my heart as he shifts his attention to the screen, and the image of the A'kai words across Violet's back, matching those of his mate.

"The Lycaons have no love for the A'kai, but they do not trust your people," I tell him. "We must go to them—seek out an alliance like we now have with the Mosaurans. Then, together, we will hunt the A'kai, and we will end them."

CHAPTER 38

VIOLET

When I open my eyes, it's to an unfamiliar room. Shiny, reflective metal panels line the ceiling, and as I turn to one side, I notice Al'iro asleep in the chair beside my bed with his hand still in mine.

I try to sit up, but I feel a bit weak. Instead, I squeeze his hand.

His eyes snap open. "Violet?"

"Where are we?" I ask softly.

"We're on the ship with my people. You were hurt. You've been asleep here in the med bay for the past several days." His voice is thick with emotion as tears fill his eyes. "We were not sure you would recover."

I reach out and cup his cheek. His golden eyes hold mine a moment before he leans in and gently brushes his lips against my own.

When he pulls back, he drops his forehead to mine. "I missed your eyes and your beautiful smile... more than you know," he whispers. "I was so afraid—"

I press a finger to his lips to silence him. "I'm fine, my love."

"Violet?" a voice calls out behind him, and I smile as Alana moves to my side. Al'iro pulls back to give her space, and she leans in to embrace me warmly. "Thank goodness you're awake. We were so worried about you."

Lara comes up beside her, and I smile at them both. Tears fill my eyes. "I was so afraid I'd never see you again."

"We were, too," Alana replies.

"I was with Elain. We escaped the A'kai, but they chased us and..."

Alana nods. "Al'iro told us. He said one of the Lycaons went to find her."

"Luken—their Alpha," Lara adds. "I met him shortly after Markus first found me. Markus says he is a good person, and that if Luken found her, he has no doubt they're both safe."

It gives me some comfort to know this, but I still worry. "Have they found any trace of them?"

Alana shakes her head. "Not yet. Vorek and I are going to go speak with the Lycaons about an alliance, but our people have been searching for them anyway."

"Good," I tell her. "I just hope they're all right."

I inhale sharply as a man with glowing, green eyes comes up behind Alana. He looks so much like the A'kai, my heart hammers in my chest as I recoil in fear.

"It's all right," Alana says quickly.

Al'iro moves closer and takes my hand. He gestures to the man. "This is my friend. Commander Vorek of the V'loryns. He will not harm you."

Alana squeezes my hand to get my attention. "I know Vorek and his people appear very similar to the A'kai, but they are *not* like them. I promise. Vorek is my mate. He's a good man, Violet. I swear it to you."

Vorek bows his head. "You have nothing to fear from me

or my people. We are not like the A'kai. We want only to help you."

"Thank you," I push out through the wave of relief. "Alana said you're searching for Elain and the others."

"Yes. We send people out to search every day. So do the Mosaurans."

Another person moves closer—a Mosauran. He places his hands on Lara's shoulders and presses a kiss to her temple. "I am Markus," he says. "It is good to meet you. Tell me: how are you feeling?"

"A bit tired," I answer honestly.

"Are you hungry?" Al'iro asks. "Thirsty?"

I shake my head.

"You should eat something," Alana presses. "Even if it's only a little bit."

"All right."

She disappears and comes back with a bowl of something resembling oatmeal. When I take a tentative spoonful, I'm surprised by how good it tastes. She and Lara sit with me while I eat as Al'iro, Vorek, and Markus all talk off to the side.

Every now and then, I notice Al'iro is watching me.

When everyone finally leaves, he walks over. "Would you like me to take you to our quarters?"

Our quarters.

"Yes."

Carefully, I stand from the bed. My balance is a bit wobbly, but Al'iro offers his arm to help steady me. "Would you like me to carry you?"

I shake my head. "I can do it."

We walk out of the med bay into the hallway. I'm surprised by how immaculately clean and kept everything is. Shiny, reflective silver panels line the floors, walls, and ceiling, mirroring my image with sparkling clarity as we walk past. I notice there are no sharp edges or corners. Everything is smooth and curved.

Vines hang down the sides of some of the walls like living curtains, lending a soft feel to the otherwise sparse and utilitarian space.

When we reach the end of one hallway, he presses his palm into a slight indentation in the wall and gestures for me to do the same. The outline of a door lights up beside it, then slides open. "Now, this space is coded to recognize you," he says.

The moment we step inside, I'm surprised by how elegantly furnished it is. A large bed carved of some sort of light wood with several nature scenes sits along one wall. There is a desk and a chair, as well as a large, L-shaped sofa facing a floor-to-ceiling window to the outside. All of it intricately carved, embedded with colorful gemstones and covered with plush green cushions.

It's such a sharp contrast to the sparse minimalism outside the door that I frown.

As if recognizing my question, he offers. "I moved several pieces of furniture from my ship over here when we allied ourselves with the V'loryns."

My gaze turns again to the floor-to ceiling window. The view of the snow-covered landscape and mountains around us is majestic and beautiful in the same breath.

He moves up behind me. The warmth of his body radiates to mine, and I'm suddenly nervous as he stands there without speaking, like the air between us is charged with some sort of electricity.

I turn to him and take his hand. "Are you sure?"

His golden eyes search mine. "What do you mean?"

"About me?" I ask, my cheeks heating in embarrassment. "About us?"

His expression softens and he cups my chin, tipping my

face up to his. "I have never been more certain of anything in my life."

A smile crests my lips. My happiness turns into awe when he spreads his wings wide for me to see the softly glowing purple color. "Your wings… they're not broken anymore, and they're glowing."

He takes my other hand and drops to one knee before me. "You are my Al'essa. I knew you were mine from the beginning. Even if you were not, I would still desire you as my mate." His gaze holds mine intently. "I offer myself to you. Please, Violet, choose me as yours. I long more than anything to be your mate."

Happiness blooms in my chest. "I choose you, Al'iro. I want to be yours."

He stands, sweeping me off my feet and into his arms. Gathering me close, he presses his lips to mine in a claiming kiss, stealing the breath from my lungs.

He takes me to the bed, gently laying me down beneath the covers. As he moves over me, I notice how careful he is to keep his weight off my body, bracing his arms on either side of me as he settles over my form.

He kisses me long and deep, and all my earlier fatigue vanishes, replaced by need so intense it burns through me like fire.

I trace my hands down the powerful muscles lining his chest to his abdomen. I dip my fingers beneath the waistband of his pants, and he stills then pulls back slightly. "You are still recovering," he whispers.

I cup his cheek. "I want you," I murmur. "I want to be yours."

He drops his forehead gently to mine. "I long to bind you to me in the ways of my people, but—"

"The mating flight," I whisper, and his eyes snap to mine. "You said that's how it's done among your people."

189

"Yes, but you are—"

I smile. "I feel fine."

With a slight clench of his jaw, he rolls us both to the side and pulls me to his chest. "I don't want to hurt you."

I sit up on my elbow and meet his gaze evenly. "If Lara can bond to Markus, and Alana to Vorek, we will be fine."

He touches my face, his eyes full of love and devotion. "You are my heart, Violet. I long more than anything to bind you to me. But I would see you fully recovered first before pressing my needs upon you, my Al'essa."

My heart melts at his words.

He's so considerate of me, in all things.

I brush my lips to his. "What if I rest tonight and we get married tomorrow?"

A devastatingly handsome smile curves his mouth. "Yes."

CHAPTER 39

AL'IRO

Vorek stands by my side as I wait for Violet to emerge from the ship. Normally, Aerilon weddings take place at night, when all the plants are lit with beautiful and vibrant bioluminescence. But here on this world, the nights can be dangerous and much colder— too cold for my Al'essa.

The sun's rays peak over the mountains beyond, casting a warm glow across the snow-covered landscape.

Everyone is here to witness our bonding ceremony. I see Violet walking toward me in her long, white, fur dress. She is so beautiful, my heart stops momentarily. I can hardly believe she chose me as hers. I do not understand what I have done to deserve such a blessing from the Creator. She is perfect, my Al'essa, and I will treasure her. Always.

When she reaches my side, a stunning smile curves her lips as she stares up at me, and I return it with one of my own. I take both her hands in mine, and we turn to face Vorek.

As my closest friend, I have asked him to preside over our ceremony.

He places his hands over ours and bows his head, reciting the blessing of the bonding ceremony as I instructed him.

When he is finished, I gently press my forehead to hers and begin the low, trilling hum in the back of my throat, signaling the end of the ceremony. The rest of my people join in and Violet and the others do their best to mimic the sound. I cannot help the smile that curves my lips at their efforts.

Vorek and Alana and Markus and Lara move closer to us as we begin to hum louder. Normally, this is only reserved for close family members, to surround us in this way, but as I look at the others, I realize Vorek is family to me—as close to me as a brother.

My eyes turn to Markus, and despite the fact that he is Mosauran, we are now family, as well. His mate considers mine her sister, just as she does Alana.

It seems the Terrans have bound us all together, in not only an alliance but in something much closer.

I look to each of them as I speak the sacred words. "A Clan is only as strong as its weakest member. Let this harmony signal the unbreakable bond that binds us together."

Vorek continues the rest of the blessing. "Take shelter beneath each other's wings, and if one of you falters, the others will share in, and carry, your burden. You are no longer just one, you are many, and there is strength in the bonding of family."

Happiness blooms in my chest, filling me with warmth. Emotions lodge in my throat as my gaze travels over each of them before landing upon my mate.

I lift Violet into my arms and extend my wings. The mating flight is about trust—the female entrusting the male to carry her as they consummate the bond. That Violet trusts me to fly us, I already know; I have carried her many times, but I never cease to be in awe and feel honored that she trusts me this much after everything she has been through.

Carefully, I take off, and we begin our ascent into the sky. Anticipation courses through me. As soon as we are above the cloud line and free of watching eyes, I kiss her long and deep while unfastening my fur robe.

She moans as I gently part the front seam of her dress and find her completely bare beneath. She wraps her legs around my hips. The warmth of her center, and the scent of her arousal, are almost more than I can bear.

My lvost lengthens and extends from my body, hard and erect between us. "Are you certain?" I whisper.

CHAPTER 40

VIOLET

I *'ve never been more certain of anything.*

"Yes," I whisper against his lips.

He lifts me in his arms, closing his mouth over my breast. He laves his tongue across the sensitive peak as I run my fingers through his hair.

He holds me close with one arm, while tracing his hand down my body to my already slick folds.

I gasp as he brushes his thumb over the small bundle of nerves at the cleft. "I want you inside me," I breathe into his ear. "Now."

Without hesitation, he aligns the crown of his lvost with my entrance.

His gaze holds mine, and the breath stutters from my lungs as he slowly enters me.

I moan at the sensation of being completely filled by him.

A low groan escapes him as he seats himself fully inside me, and for a moment, he forgets our flight. We begin spiraling downward before his sudden realization of what is happening.

Quickly, he recovers. A low growl rumbles in his chest as his golden eyes pin me in place. "You're so tight," he rasps.

A small pinch of pain deep inside makes me gasp, but it's followed quickly by pleasure. "What is—"

"My stem," he reminds me. "Attaching to your womb."

A moan escapes my lips as a pleasurable warmth blooms in my core. I've never made love before, but already my body begins to tighten around his lvost.

"Al'iro," I murmur. "You feel so good."

He rolls his hips against mine as pleasure coils tightly within.

His gaze holds mine, and my mouth falls open as the warmth turns into an intense heat expanding deep inside me. Waves of pleasure move over and through me, and I cry out his name as I find my release.

His lvost pulses inside me and he roars out, "Mine!" as we fall over the edge together into blissful oblivion.

As I come back down from my pleasure, he carefully withdraws, and I already miss the feel of him inside me. He lands on a mountain ledge, and I frown at him. "Where are we?"

"The Mosaurans were kind enough to tell me about this pod," he says, pressing his palm to the panel and walking us inside. "This one is surrounded by a force shield," he says as he presses a button on the inner panel, and the walls disappear so it looks as though we're outside.

I notice the shimmering reflection of the clear force shield, glad of the extra protection.

I don't have time to take in everything as he moves us to the bed, and gently lays me down atop a nest of white furs.

He settles over me, sealing his mouth over my own in a

searing kiss. His tongue curls around mine, and when he finally pulls back, I'm breathless and panting beneath him.

"I must have you again," he whispers against my lips.

He kisses a heated trail along my jaw and down my neck to my left breast, closing his mouth over the peak. I moan, and arch up against him. He turns his attention to the other breast, and then moves down my body.

Gently, he parts my legs. His nostrils flare and his golden gaze meets mine, full of intense possession. "I will fill you with my essence many times, my beautiful Al'essa, so that every male within several *arcums* will know you are mine."

My toes curl in anticipation as he dips his head between my thighs and drags his tongue through my folds. When he reaches the small bundle of nerves at the top, I dig my heels into his back and cry out his name.

It doesn't take long for me to climax, and when I do, stars burst behind my eyes.

I'm not even recovered from my orgasm when he moves back up my body and aligns his lvost with my entrance.

He groans as he pushes into me, fully seating himself deep in my core.

The friction of his lvost in my channel is exquisite as each stroke becomes longer, deeper, and more forceful.

My head falls back as ecstasy moves through me.

He cups my chin. "I want to watch you as you find your release," he growls.

I run my hands over his back, enjoying the flex of his muscles beneath my fingers as he thrusts deep inside me.

The small pinch of pain as his stem enters my womb is quickly replaced by intense pleasure.

I tighten my legs around him, relishing the sensation as he continues to pump into me.

He wraps his hand around my hip, holding me in place, his golden eyes staring deep into mine.

My lips part as wave after wave of pleasure washes over and through me. My release triggers his own, and his lvost begins to pulse in my core as intense warmth erupts deep within. He cries out my name as he fills me again with his seed.

He drops down and kisses me long and deep before rolling us so that he's on his back beneath me. He sits up, wrapping his arms and wings around my form, holding me close as he moves his hips against mine. "You want me again so soon?"

"Always, my beautiful Al'essa." He seals his mouth over mine, and pulls me even closer.

I hold tightly to him, feeling the beat of his heart against my own as he thrusts up into me. Nothing exists outside of this moment with him and the feel of our bodies joined as one.

"I love you," I whisper against his lips.

"You are mine, Violet," he breathes in reply. "And I am yours."

CHAPTER 41

AL'IRO

When I wake in the morning, Violet is asleep in my arms. We made love several times last night, and I would have made love to her several more, but my mate became tired. Gently, I brush the hair back from her face and press a tender kiss to her lips to awaken her.

Her eyelids flutter and open, and she gives me a sleepy smile. I wrap my arms and wings around her and roll her beneath me, sealing my mouth over hers, kissing her long and deep.

When I pull back, she touches my face, her hazel eyes staring deep into mine. I love her so much my heart feels as if it will burst. I lean down to kiss her again, but movement outside our pod catches my attention.

I snap my head up, and my eyes go wide as I see a Lycaon carrying a Terran female.

I recognize Luken immediately.

Violet's gaze follows mine, and she gasps. "Elain!"

Quickly, we dress and move to the door. I hand Violet a blaster and take one as a precaution. "Stay behind me," I tell her.

She nods, and we exit the pod.

Luken's eyes meet mine, their normally glowing, orange color dim instead of bright. His gaze drops to the female in his arms, her entire body limp. "She needs help," he says weakly. "Please, you must save her."

"What happened?"

His eyes roll up in the back of his head, and he drops to his knees on the ground. He twists at the last moment so as not to fall onto her as he holds her to his chest.

Violet rushes to her friend. "Elain!"

I tap on my wrist comm to contact our people, praying it works.

A moment later, Vorek's face appears in the viewscreen. "Send someone to our pod, right away! We have found Luken and Elain. They are injured and unconscious. Hurry!"

He dips his chin, and the screen goes blank.

I kneel beside them both, running a scanner over them. The marks on their necks tell me what happened: they were bitten by an A'kai.

Panic snakes down my spine. I turn to Violet. "Get back in the pod. I will bring them inside."

"I can help you," she protests.

"No," I snap, as my gaze scans the woods. "They were bitten by an A'kai. He may still be nearby."

Violet returns to the pod while I quickly drag Elain and Luken inside. I slam my hand on the panel to reactivate the force shield.

While we wait for help to arrive, I run the scanner over them again. Worry fills me as I study Elain's readings. "Your friend has lost much blood, but she will live."

"What about him?"

"Lycaons are like my people. A'kai venom renders them unconscious. He should recover, in time."

I scan our surroundings again. "We must leave this place, and return to our territory. It is not safe to remain here."

I clench my jaw as frustration burns through me. I should never have brought my mate out here. We should have stayed at the ship.

In the distance, I notice four of my people flying toward us. I scan outside once more to check for danger, and then lower the shield.

I open the door just as they land beside us. "We must hurry," I tell En'oro. "They were bitten by an A'kai, and I do not know how close he may be."

They gather Elain and Luken while I pull Violet into my arms. My wings beat furiously as we fly back to our territory. I am desperate to return my mate to the safety of our ship.

As soon as we land, the others rush to greet us.

"What happened?" Vorek asks.

"An A'kai bit them."

His gaze drops to the female. "Will she live?"

"Yes."

Alana follows us to the med bay, and we place them each in an MRU.

"How long will they be unconscious?" Vorek asks.

I study the readings on the display. "Luken should awaken in a few hours. As for Elain, I am uncertain."

I glance at Alana—Vorek's mate—hoping she will know more. As a Terran Healer, she is more familiar with their anatomy than I am.

Her eyes are bright with tears as she looks to her friend. "It is hard to tell. The MRUs are not programmed for our species. My best estimation is anywhere from six to twelve hours, according to this reading."

～

It has been several hours. Elain and Luken are still unconscious in the Med Bay.

As I hold my mate in my arms, my thoughts keep returning to them. I know they will be fine, but it makes me worry for my own mate. That could so easily have been her.

The A'kai are dangerous. They will continue to hunt the Terrans, unless we end them.

Alarms begin blaring throughout the ships, startling Violet awake. Her eyes are wide as they meet mine. "What's happening?"

I hit my wrist comm and contact Vorek. "What is going on?"

He clenches his jaw. "Luken and Elain—they are gone."

"What? How?"

"I do not know. Healer En'oro said he was only out of the Med Bay for a few minutes. When he returned, they were gone. The vidcam feed shows Luken carrying the female away from the ship and back out into the forest."

He runs a hand roughly through his hair. "Why would he take her away from the safety of our vessel?"

"Because the Lycaons do not trust you," I state bluntly. "They believe your race is like the A'kai. He must have thought she was in danger. He is probably taking her to his people."

Vorek sighs heavily. "We have to find them. If the A'kai locate them first, they will be in trouble. I'll send out a search."

I nod as the display cuts off.

Violet turns to me, worry etched in her features. "She's probably so scared, Al'iro. How could he just take her like that?"

"Luken probably believes he is saving her from danger.

He would never hurt her, Violet. It is not their way. You know this."

"I'm just worried. It's a long way from here to his people. What if they run into another A'kai?"

I am concerned about this as well. We still do not have an exact number of how many A'kai are now on this planet.

Encountering even one A'kai can be dangerous. If Luken were to have to fight off several, I doubt he would be able to defend Elain, and live.

"We'll find them, Violet." I pull her close to my chest, and smooth a hand down her back in a soothing gesture. "We will not stop searching until we do."

EPILOGUE

AL'IRO

It has been several days since Luken stole the Terran female away. We have searched but have not yet found them.

When one of the Mosaurans traveled to the location of their cave, they refused to grant him entrance. He claims he could scent the Terran female with them.

Violet and I have decided to go to them. We leave tomorrow to speak to the Lycaons. It is my hope we can convince them she will be safe with us and the V'loryns.

I am reluctant to travel with my mate, especially now that I suspect something I need to discuss with her.

Violet turns in my arms to face me, cupping my cheek. "When we made love earlier, it was… different," she says softly. "I didn't feel your stem like I normally do."

With slight tension in my face, I lower my gaze as guilt fills me. I should have realized this could happen, and now, I fear she will be angry with me if my suspicions are correct. "I must scan you, Violet. I believe you may be carrying our fledgling."

Her small brow furrows. "What?"

"Our stem does not attach to the womb when a female is carrying." I pause. "Please, may I scan you to be sure?"

Her eyes widen slightly as she nods. Carefully, I run the scanner over her abdomen.

My heart squeezes in my chest as I study the read out. She is, indeed, carrying my child.

"Is that... what I think it is?" she asks, pointing to the small spot on the screen.

Reluctantly, I nod, my happiness cut off by the guilt of knowing I should have taken precautions against this. She may not even want a fledgling, yet.

Or at all.

Tears fill her eyes, and devastation washes through me. "Forgive me, Violet. I should have known this could happen. I should have been more careful. Are you upset?"

A tear rolls gently down her cheek as she turns her hazel eyes to me. "No," she whispers. "I'm happy."

A smile crests my lips. "Truly?"

I place my hand on her lower abdomen, my heart so full of joy I feel as though it will burst.

"Yes." She smiles, and it is brighter than the very sun itself.

She places her hand over mine on her belly. In her eyes, I can see our future. I curl my wings around her, and repeat my solemn vow. "Whatever fate awaits us, we will meet it together, my beautiful Al'essa."